ELIZABETH JOHNS

With the Wind

A SERIES OF ELEMENTS BOOK THREE

To Jill, Julie, and Rebekah who have known loss too young

ELIZABETH JOHNS

A SERIES OF ELEMENTS BOOK THREE

Prologue

"This is the first time we will be apart," Beaujolais announced sadly to her triplet sisters, who were sitting with her on a large canopied bed in their London town house. They were enjoying their nightly ritual of gathering in Margaux's room. Anjou, Beaujolais, and Margaux were the identical beautiful daughters of the Marquess of Ashbury and his French Marchioness.

"It is not forever, dear," Margaux said soothingly as she brushed her sister's long ebony locks to a silky sheen. "We will be together again. There will be house parties and holidays…"

"It was bound to happen sooner or later. I thought we would all be married by now. Yet, here we are, on the shelf!" Beaujolais exclaimed.

"I am happy to be claiming my space on the shelf if it means leaving the Marriage Mart! You must admit I have lost the ability to hold my tongue. It is best I leave before I ruin you all," Margaux said laughingly.

"Yes, dear, we know. But a convent? Did you truly think *Maman* would allow it?" Anjou asked sceptically as she flashed her brilliant blue eyes at her sister.

"No. At least they are allowing me to go to help with the orphanage in Scotland," Margaux replied, apparently satisfied with her lot.

"I would wager *Maman* will have you back here in less than three months," Anjou taunted while she mindlessly twisted her hair about her finger.

"I accept." Margaux held out her hand to shake on it, never one to shun sisterly competition.

"Stop, you two," Beaujolais said with disgust. "Could you not be happy here? Could you not beg *Maman* to simply let you stay at home?"

Margaux shook her head. "As if our *maman*, grandest hostess in the kingdom, would allow her single daughter to waste away at home. But even so, it would not be enough. I want freedom, dear. Can you try to understand?"

Tears welled up in Beaujolais' eyes, causing their violet hue to deepen. "I'm sorry, Marg. I will try to be happy for you, but I cannot understand it."

Margaux sighed. "You are the one born to be a duchess, Jolie. I will leave brilliant marriages to the two of you."

"Do not tease me about being a duchess. Besides, there are only two unmarried dukes in the kingdom. One is ancient and the other a recluse."

"Afraid we will curse you?" Anjou joined in taunting with her other sister. Since they were small, it had long been a source of amusement to tease Beaujolais. She had pretended to be a duchess when they had played as children, and acted the most like one. It had not helped that their mother had encouraged it.

"You *have* already turned down at least a baronet, a mister, two earls, and a marquess," Margaux pointed out helpfully.

"None could be taken seriously! And both of you have had as many offers as I," Beaujolais insisted in her own defence.

"*I* have not," Anjou boasted.

"And neither of us professes to be open to *marriage de convenance*," Margaux added.

"That is because you do not allow anyone to propose to you," Beaujolais retorted.

"I cannot consider anyone else," Anjou said looking away.

Margaux took her hand to comfort her. "It has been years without word of Aidan, Anj. Do you not think it is time to forget him?" she asked kindly.

Anjou shook her head and allowed her tears to spill down her face. "I need to do something. I cannot wait much longer for Father's enquiries." She stepped down from the bed and began to pace as she wiped her tears away. Her love, Aidan, had gone off to the American war and had not been heard from since the hostilities had ended.

"What do you propose to do?" Jolie asked with a frown.

"I want to go and look for him."

"Go and look for him?" Her sisters spoke simultaneously in disbelief.

Anjou nodded. "Charles has agreed to help me." Their brother, Charles, and Aidan had been best friends.

"*Maman* and *Papa* will never agree to that."

"They have and they will," Anjou answered quietly without looking at her sisters. "As soon as Father's enquiries are complete."

Beaujolais cried in earnest then. "It truly is the last time we will all be together!"

None of the sisters argued, but enveloped one another in a hug, wondering how life would change without the other parts of themselves.

Chapter One

"*Maman, Papa*," Anjou said to her parents when she found them alone together in the drawing room. She had finally worked up the courage to speak to them about something she had at last resolved to do.

"What is it, Anjou?" her father asked.

"I need to go to America," she blurted out.

Her parents exchanged a look.

"I still have investigators looking for Aidan, my dear. It is not safe to let you go to America alone," her father tried to reason with her.

"But for how much longer, *Papa*?" she asked, making no effort to mask her frustration.

"Until you are satisfied he is no longer alive," he answered with a frown.

"Charles has agreed to go with me." She stood as she argued her case.

"Has he?" her father asked with an arch look. "I wonder that he did not think to consult with me first."

"*Papa*," she said quietly, "Do not be cross with Charles. I am not brave enough to go alone, and I asked him to accompany me before I came to you. I must do this. I do not *want* to do this, but I must."

"Why we ever agreed to let you and Aidan do this, I cannot remember," her mother said with regret.

"*Maman*, you love Aidan as much as I. I know there is but a small chance I will find him alive, but it needs to be done. I cannot go on with my life until I know for certain."

"Where do you mean to stay? How do you mean to get there? Have you thought of the realities of travelling across an ocean to an unknown land?" her father objected rather harshly.

"Charles has a friend who captains a ship back and forth on a regular basis. He is going to take us to Virginia to the Eastons' plantation. I had hoped to make contact with your investigators to see what they have discovered, and where they have already looked for him." She continued to press her case as her parents listened to her well-considered reasoning. "I thought, perhaps, if he looks different, or is injured somewhere, I might be able to recognise him when they cannot."

"You have been thinking of this a great deal," her father remarked.

"I have thought of little else for four years," she said quietly. "I have tried to consider him as dead and think of other suitors, but I cannot."

Her mother put her hands to her head and shook it back and forth. "I do not want you to go. Can Charles not go alone? He was his best friend—he could certainly recognise him."

"But I am his wife."

"No one else knows, Anjou," her mother protested.

Her father let out a sigh. "An error in judgement I continue to regret. You do not require our permission to go."

"I would prefer to have it, just the same."

Her father paused for some time, and she thought he would refuse. At last he gave a reluctant nod.

~*~

Anjou was terrified. She had never before crossed an ocean. She was not brave like her sisters, but she could not carry on with her life until she was certain. Her mind told her that Aidan could not be alive after four years, but her heart knew she must search for him. She had never sailed further than across the Channel from France to England, and she

9

did not want to be on a boat now any more than she had then. If her brother Charles had not agreed to accompany her, she would have turned back by now.

She stood on the dock, watching as cargo was loaded onto the ship. The Isle of Wight, a short journey away, caused her to consider the distance she was about to travel with deepening dismay. The air was thick and hot, and the only relief from the smells of rotten fish and salty water was an occasional breeze. She prayed it would not smell so strongly the entire journey. Charles had told her there would be no other women aboard, save herself and her maid, so she feared the worst in that regard.

"Can I help you, miss?" asked a man in the deep voice of a gentleman. Anjou was startled, as she was lost in thought.

"I beg your pardon. I did not mean to frighten you, but a lady should not be left alone on the docks."

She looked upward to see a large man towering over her. He was sun-weathered, with several days' beard, but she could not make out his eyes for the sun's glare and the shadow of his hat.

"I am not alone. I am with my brother and my maid. He was searching for someone to load our trunks," she replied, feeling unaccountably comfortable around this stranger, to whom she had not been introduced.

"Onto the *Wind*?" he asked doubtfully.

"Is that the name of this ship?" she asked, for some odd reason forgetting his question and smiling.

"Her full name is *With the Wind*, but we call her *Wind* for short." His eyes twinkled with amusement.

"It was meant to be, then," she said, as she looked at the large, wooden vessel with tall poles, and sails and ropes, which was somehow supposed to remain upright on the ocean. She resolved to be less afraid if this was her destiny.

"What was meant to be?" he asked suspiciously.

"My trip to America." She considered him more closely, wondering why it would matter to him. His eyes were a strange colour of greyish-green, and were very disconcerting when they were examining her from head to toe.

"Might I be so bold as to ask who your brother is?"

"Charles Winslow. He is a friend of the Captain."

"He is, is he?"

"Are you going to introduce yourself, then?" she asked, growing impatient with his questions.

"Edward Harris, at your service." He removed his hat and proffered an elegant bow. He replaced his hat on his head and continued, "Captain of the *Wind*."

"I am…"

He interrupted. "I know exactly who you are, my lady, and I am not at all happy about it."

~*~

Charles returned from overseeing the loading of their trunks on board the ship, but he did not receive the greeting he normally would have anticipated from an old friend.

"Winslow. Follow me now." Edward turned and marched off without waiting for a response. He walked towards the boat, out of earshot of Anjou.

"A pleasure to see you, too," Charles muttered from behind as he followed.

"What is the meaning of this? You did not mention your sister. I distinctly remember you said Andrew was the passenger. I never would have agreed to have a lady on my ship," Captain Harris said as he stopped and spun around to face Charles.

"No. I said Anjou."

"Anjou. Andrew." He cursed, clearly realising the similarity. "Well, she cannot go."

"You cannot just tell her no when she has finally worked up the courage to do so!"

"Oh, I can. And I will." He moved, with the apparent intention of doing just that, but was stopped when Charles took his arm.

"You do not understand," Charles said quietly.

"I understand perfectly. Do you know how bawdy sailors get when they are weeks without a woman? Having her on board is akin to Satan dangling an apple in front of Eve. Forbidden fruit." He held up his hand as if holding something tantalizing in front of Charles's face. "I would not subject any mother or sister of mine to it. Not to mention all the superstitions about having a woman on board. It is bad luck."

"You cannot control your men for six weeks?"

"I run a tight ship, but this is not an easy life and this craft is very small when you've nowhere else to go. The crew are not used to having ladies on board, and I am fairly certain your sister would not wish to be subjected to any of it."

"I will be responsible for her," Charles said defensively as he stood taller.

"Deuced right you will, but here in England." He began walking away.

"Aidan," Charles said by way of explanation, causing Harris to pause.

"As in Gardiner?"

"Indeed. He is her husband."

Edward looked away for a moment as he appeared to digest the information. "A very sad ending to a fine gentleman, but what does it have to do with your sister wanting to go to America?"

"He was never found. She feels she needs to find him herself before she can get on with her life."

"Do you have any idea how large America is? How widespread the war there was? It is not the same as looking in Spain or France. She could look for the rest of her life and never search the half of it," Edward said with a shake of his head.

"I know, and you know, but she needs to understand for herself. I do not wish her to grow old wondering. She deserves the chance, and I mean to see she gets it."

Edward shook his head again and crossed his large arms over his chest. "She will have to find another way. It is a very bad idea."

"Captain Harris?" Anjou's voice spoke from behind the burly seaman, who shut his eyes in obvious frustration. Anjou was not going to make this easy for Edward.

Charles wondered how much she had heard.

"Yes, my lady," Edward said as he spun around to face her. Even from another yard's distance, Charles could see her bright blue eyes were sparkling with unshed tears.

"What can I say to make you change your mind?" she asked quietly.

"Lady Anjou, you do not understand how this would be for you. A merchant ship is no place for a gently bred female. Have your brother seek passage for you on a packet ship meant to accommodate ladies," Edward said, with surprising kindness, instead of the derisive manner Charles would have expected.

"I understand, and I promise to keep out of the way of you and your men. Your ship goes faster than the passenger ones, and I want to go as quickly as possible."

"And why is that?" he asked. There was a hint of curiosity in his voice.

"I do not want to be on the ship any longer than I have to. Please allow me passage, sir. I do not think I can work up the courage to try again if you say no."

Edward looked out over the water and drew a long, slow breath. He began to walk away and then stopped and ran his fingers through his hair.

"Get on the ship. Before I change my mind."

Anjou felt her brother tug on her arm and he started leading her to the gangplank. The boat seemed too small to her when she saw all of the burly seamen swarming on it. None of them looked as if they knew what a bath or a razor was. Some ogled, some spat, and some whistled—to a harsh "Belay!" from their captain.

Silence followed the command, so she supposed it meant something dreadful. She looked upward at the miles of ropes and the tall poles that seemed to sway to and fro. How was this supposed to remain upright in the water?

She had already concluded she would be left behind, and now she could not think well enough to put one foot in front of the other. It did not help that her legs were shaking either. Charles seemed to understand her apprehension and hurried her onto the ship and down into a tiny cabin, with wood-paneled walls and only a lantern for light.

She could feel the boat wobble beneath her feet and she clutched the nearest nailed-down post she could reach. She closed her eyes and silently repeated *Aidan, Aidan, Aidan,* to remind herself and firm her resolve. She opened her eyes again and took a look around her. The room was smaller than any of the servants' quarters at her parents' residences. There was a small bunk with her trunk placed nearby, and there was a hammock strung from hooks.

Her brother was still holding her other arm. "Are you certain you can do this? There is no turning back once we set sail."

Anjou looked up at her brother, whose ebony locks and blue eyes mirrored her own, and who was gazing at her with tender concern. She nodded as she took a handkerchief from her reticule and covered her nose. The smell near the docks had been one of rotten fish and dirty water. It was akin to a damp cellar and she looked around for a way to air the space.

"Where is the window?" she asked.

"No windows, except in the Captain's quarters, but he owns the ship. You can step out with Hannah or myself when you need fresh air—just never alone, understand? I believe I'm in a cabin with Edward. Can I leave you for a while? I need to ensure my own trunk arrived. I will send Hannah to you."

She nodded again, and fell to her knees in tears the moment the door closed behind him.

"How am I to do this? But how can I not?"

She grasped the locket around her neck, which held her thin wedding band and the only portrait she had of Aidan. His youthful face and stark black eyes looked up at her, full of innocence and life. It had been years since anyone had seen or heard of him; even the War Office considered him lost in battle.

She squeezed her eyes tight and tried to remember his scent, his touch, but she could not, no matter how hard she tried. She panicked and flung open her trunk, tossing her belongings to and fro whilst searching for a box. When she found it, she tore the lid open and held one of the beloved letters it contained to her nose to recapture his scent. It was faint, but enough to calm her panic.

"Yes, that is him," she whispered.

She sat on the small bunk and, burying her face in her hands, began to laugh nervously.

"I have gone mad before we even set sail."

She lay in peace for a few minutes, listening to the creaks and groans of the *Wind*, and long enough to regain her composure, though she could hear the crew shouting and chanting as the boat began to move. She daydreamed of the first time she had met Aidan. He had come home from school with Charles for a school holiday, and she had shied away from strangers as she always did. However, as the days passed, she found herself watching him from behind her viola or book, curious to know him. He was gentle and quiet, which suited Anjou's own timid introversion. He was a calming, secure presence, even though he had been little more than a boy when he had left for the war.

The first time she remembered speaking to Aidan, she had been sitting by the river, lost in a book.

She had looked up to see him standing in his breeches with no stockings, and a trout dangling on the end of his line.

He was gentle even in fishing; he pulled in the fish with ease. When at last he turned to see her, he smiled kindly. "Good day, Lady Anjou. I did not realise you were reading there. Pardon my intrusion."

"How did you know which one I was?"

He thought for a moment. "I just do. You are different from your sisters."

"I am." She hung her head a bit, feeling that it was a weakness.

With a few quiet strides through the water, he was by her side. He knelt down and lifted her chin.

"I intended it as a compliment."

"You did?" she asked doubtfully. "But my sisters are much more vibrant and pleasing."

"Not to me," he said softly. "Beauty is different to everyone."

She blushed and looked away, noticing his fish.

"Why do you like to fish?" she asked uncharacteristically, for she was normally afraid of strangers—even if he was a friend of Charles.

"Why do you like to read?" he asked with a sly grin, indicating he knew he had answered a question with a question.

She thought for a moment before answering. "I like to escape. I do not need constant activity as my sisters seem to. I enjoy being alone and having quiet."

"It is the same for me with fishing."

"It seems rather a bore. And are the fish not slimy?"

"Would you like to try it?"

She was hardly expecting that reply. "I- I suppose I could."

He stood and held out his hand to assist her from the ground.

"You had best tie up your skirts, unless you prefer to be wet."

"Oh, I could not! My mother would know I had escaped my lessons!"

"I will not look. I promise."

He turned his back while she tied her skirts to her knees and stepped into the shallow water. He handed her a pole and the hook that dangled from a line of string.

"Hold that for a moment while I fetch the bait."

When he stepped into the water near her, he was dangling a worm from his fingers.

She simply stared at it.

"Go on, take it," he said as he held it a little closer to her. She swallowed with trepidation but did not want to show him how afraid she was.

She took the worm and tried not to think about what she was holding in her hand as it twisted and writhed around.

"Now you place it on the hook."

He spared her and showed her how when he looked up and saw her face.

"Next, you put it in the water and you wait for a bite."

She obeyed and watched as he baited his hook and placed it some distance from hers.

They stood in silent tranquility for some time, listening and feeling the water gently rush by.

After some minutes, or perhaps even an hour, she felt a tug on her line.

"I think I might have something," she exclaimed.

"Pull your line in," he instructed.

As she pulled and the object grew closer she felt a rush of exhilaration and accomplishment.

Unfortunately, the fish was too small to keep.

Aidan patiently showed her how to take the fish off the hook without cutting herself. She was too excited to realise he was standing directly behind her and his hands were on hers.

"It is most definitely slimy," she said, though she did it.

He laughed and then grew quiet, with a look at her that made her realise she was not a child in his eyes, and perhaps he saw her as more than the bothersome younger sister of his friend. Her heart began to beat faster and her breathing changed. She suddenly realised she was vulnerable to this man, but she was not afraid of him. She stared back into those dark eyes as he reached up and brushed a stray hair from her cheek.

"You had best return to your lessons," he whispered breathlessly.

"Yes, I should," she said, his words snapping her out of her daze. "Thank you for teaching me to fish."

"It was my pleasure, my lady." He looked at her, his happiness now turned to sadness.

"Perhaps we may fish again before you return to Oxford?"

"I will fish again with you on the morrow, if you are able to meet me here."

She nodded with nervous anticipation, having spent the most glorious afternoon in her remembrance, although she knew her parents would not approve. "I will be here."

He bent down to retrieve her book and blanket while she untangled her skirts, then handed them to her. Their hands brushed and she felt a strange sensation of pleasure rush through her that she had never known before. She smiled and walked away, wondering what it all could mean.

She heard a knock on her door. Before answering, she brushed away a tear which had fallen.

Hannah entered, and her brown eyes grew wide as she studied the mess Anjou had made of the trunk and took in the small surroundings.

"Is there something you need, my lady? Where am I to unpack your trunk? There is scarcely room to turn about in here!"

"I found what I wanted. It seems there is no unpacking. It is you, our trunks, and me."

"Very well. I will go and see if I can at least find a basin or some water for you to wash with," Hannah answered, a frown marring her normally placid countenance.

Anjou nodded, and Charles entered as the maid left.

Chapter Two

"How do you do thus far?" Charles questioned.

Anjou sighed derisively. "Has it been two hours, Charles?"

"I suppose I was making small-talk." He chuckled. "Do you mean to stay in this tiny cabin the entire journey?"

"I believe I will. The Captain obviously does not appreciate my presence on board," she said with uncharacteristic petulance.

"Do not worry about Edward. He has not been around ladies in years."

"Perhaps that is a blessed thing," she muttered.

"Nevertheless, you cannot stay in the cabin for weeks."

"You, of all people, know I do not mind my own company."

"True, but there is a reason the term cabin fever arose. You cannot remain in a small, dark room with no windows for over a month."

She twisted her lips sideways. "Mayhap I will go about with you when the Captain is sleeping."

"That could be difficult. I have never met anyone who needed so little sleep as Edward Harris. However, I will try to accommodate you. I cannot say I would be too keen myself, after what he said on shore, but he is a great fellow at heart—known him since school days. He has not had an easy time of it, so the gruff exterior is somewhat understandable."

"What do you mean?" Anjou asked with infuriating curiosity about the handsome Captain, even if she was irritated by his treatment of her. She was an observer of people, which she attributed to her shy nature. He was most definitely a gentleman, no matter how he disguised it. Why had she felt initially comfortable with him?

"I mean he comes from excellent stock, but his wastrel father depleted the family coffers. He left home to provide for his siblings and has made an excellent living. Most people shun him for it."

"The English would. The French would applaud him."

"If they bothered to ask before they cut off his head. Anyway, I will return for you when Edward catches some sleep." Charles turned to leave but stopped. "If you do happen to bump into him, remember what I said."

"Of course. I am much more likely to duck and keep mum."

He smiled and patted the cabin door twice before closing it behind him.

Anjou thought back to her conversation with Lady Easton some time ago, when she had first toyed with the idea of going to search for Aidan herself.

"I must admit, the voyage is very long," Lady Easton had said. "We were on a very large ship that did not sail fast. There were days we did not seem to move at all! I hear there are some newly designed boats which make the journey in as little as one month! I believe they might be smaller, but it is perhaps something to consider. We had a small cabin, with a sitting room the Captain normally used for his family, though they were not travelling due to the war. I do not know how other ships might be."

"I cannot fathom an entire month on a ship," Anjou had answered with dread. "I can barely stand the short trip across the Channel."

"I, too, find the Channel crossing unpleasant sometimes," Lady Easton commiserated. "It always seems to be rough. But I am fortunate not to be affected by the sea sickness. My brother and sister are prone to it, and my maid!" She laughed as she recollected. "Poor thing—she was in her bunk almost the entire journey."

"I am more terrified than ill, I think."

"Most people find they grow used to it and feel better after a day or two."

"What can you occupy your time with?"

"I spent most of my journey nursing Lord Easton's war wounds. I do not recommend it," Lady Easton jested. "I would take medicines, however, if I were to go again, and I do long to visit my old home soon. I would pack any number of things. I did take six books, and I read each of them multiple times. Many women sew, play card games, keep a diary, or even play an instrument."

"I do love to read, and I can sew. I had not thought to take my viola."

"The captain on our ship had a love for culinary delights and we were well supplied with victuals. You must dampen your expectations, however, for I still grew weary of the same meal every third day."

"I had not thought of the food. One takes it for granted on land."

"Yes, indeed! I think fresh water was the luxury I most longed for. Where do you mean to go in America?"

Anjou had not disclosed her marriage to anyone, save her parents, at their insistence. They reasoned they wanted Aidan to come back alive, first. It made little sense to her.

"I believe I would like to see Washington," she answered vaguely.

"The capital? It is near my home, across the river in Virginia."

"Yes, I had heard."

Lady Easton looked thoughtful. "May I ask why you wish to go if you are terrified of sailing? You need not answer if I intrude."

Anjou hesitated and struggled to keep her composure.

"I promised my parents I would not tell."

"Then you need not. However, I insist you stay at my home while you are there. I will write to my old maid, Josie, who is now the housekeeper there. Her husband, Buffy, was Easton's batman in the army. He serves as our steward. They will gladly help you with anything you need."

"Anything?" she asked with surprise.

Lady Easton nodded. "Of course."

"May I speak to my parents before you send a letter? I must convince them to let me go."

"You do not intend to go alone, do you?" Lady Easton asked with a warning in her voice.

"I had supposed I would take my maid."

Lady Easton shook her head. "Absolutely not. You must not go alone. I came over with only my maid because of necessity. We were trying to outrun a war, and even though I had my family to receive me in England, there were still consequences to be had in society. I do not know why you wish to go, but I suspect you have your reasons. The Americans are wonderful people, but may be suspicious of an English woman, and especially an unmarried one travelling alone. You have no one there to receive you, and will not be able to go about in society alone."

"I had not thought so far ahead," Anjou confessed.

"I was young when we left, and have only returned once since that time, but I suspect it has changed little in that regard. I was quite a hoyden in my youth, and if it had not been for my father's protection, I would have suffered. I would suggest you take your father with you, if he is amenable."

"I suspect not," Anjou whispered, disheartened.

"Perhaps your brother?" Lady Easton suggested.

"Perhaps." She felt a rush of hope at the suggestion.

"May I tell you one thing in confidence?" she asked.

Anjou nodded.

"My sister, Sarah, is living there alone. She wished to be away from England for a time."

"Will she mind the intrusion?"

"No. There have been other visitors. The house is large enough that she may keep to herself if she wishes."

"I understand. I prefer solace most of the time myself."

Lady Easton nodded. "I suspected as much. Sarah is recovering from the violent death of her husband. It happened just before Christmas."

"Lady Abernathy?" Anjou asked with astonishment, recollecting the rumours she had heard. She had not realised the connection, though it was likely her mother had mentioned it.

"Indeed. The details of his duel and sordid affairs are widely known, unfortunately."

"I am very sorry to hear it. I will not trouble her."

"I only tell you this so you need not ask her unnecessary questions. She would not be a suitable chaperone either, as she will not go into society."

"No, of course not," Anjou agreed.

"You will let me know when you decide. It will take some time for a letter to reach them."

"I must convince my brother to accompany me, and of course my parents. I fear those obstacles will be easier than convincing myself."

"Have courage, my dear. You must think of what could happen if you do go, and what will not if you stay."

"Yes, I must remember those words. Thank you, Lady Easton."

"You are most welcome. And please, call me Elly."

Elly had done more to help her than Anjou could have imagined. Beyond the words, which finally lit the fire under her to make a decision, she had lent her all kinds of medical supplies, clothing, boots, ginger biscuits and books to aid her in the journey. Anjou had also brought some sewing projects, and her viola to keep her company. Once she grew used to the movement of the boat, she was certain she would be grateful for all the advice.

~*~

"This is almost tolerable," Charles remarked as he looked appreciatively at the Captain's lair, rubbing his hand along the mahogany panelling lining the three paned windows aft of the ship. It almost had a homely feeling. "Thank you for accommodating me."

"It is my home most of the time. It is small, but I manage. Thank you for assisting with the rigging," Edward replied, watching Charles rub his sore hands.

"I shall not make a habit of it. I might begin to look like you," the latter teased.

"Sailing is not work for a gentleman, to be sure. You may take the bunk over there," Edward said pointing to one of two beds along the sides of the cabin. A small desk and their trunks completed the room. The adjacent room was a small salon where the Captain and mates took their meals. On the other side of the bulkhead were two small state-rooms; one was shared by the mates and the other by Anjou and Hannah. They were less than half the size of this cabin, which was not more than ten feet by ten feet, including the bunks. Most of the room on a merchant ship was taken up by cargo, though some ships did have more luxurious accommodations for well-paying passengers. Even the crew rotated, sharing hammocks when they traded watch. Sailing was a twenty-four-hour operation, one which Charles had not fully appreciated until he had witnessed it first-hand. He had not exerted himself so since the battlefield.

"I am curious," Edward started to say once he had settled himself. "Your sister mentioned she chose this ship."

Charles nodded. "She spoke at length with Lady Easton about her travels. She did not think she could abide six or more weeks at sea, so she studied the papers and found out about your ship."

"While flattering, I cannot guarantee a swifter journey. It all depends on the weather, and if you asked my men right now, they will be sure her presence will curse our travels."

"She would be certain of a long journey on a packet, and she is terrified of being on a boat."

"A match made in heaven," Edward quipped. "I warned the men to leave her be."

"I do not think it will be a problem," Charles said, wondering whether or not to mention her intentions to stay in her cabin.

"I fully expected her to see her cabin and then boot me from mine, as most ladies would do," he teased.

"My sisters are tougher than they look. Anjou keeps to herself around strangers, and will do so especially now she knows you do not approve of her. She will hide away."

"You mean she plans to avoid me the entire journey?" Edward roared with laughter.

"She may be shy, but she is also very stubborn," Charles explained.

"This could be more amusing than anything in years," Edward said tapping his glass over the map on his desk.

"At ease, Captain," Charles said a little defensively, wondering what his friend could be planning for his sister.

"Worry not, my friend. I will not harm her. She might hurt herself..."

"I am greatly comforted," Charles said with a glare at his old friend.

"My cook did not make this journey because he had to attend to a sick relative. I was thinking perhaps she might be of use in the galley. Unless you enjoy eating the slops the steward makes."

Charles wrinkled his face with disgust. "I imagine you like them less than I do, if I remember your palate correctly."

"Never fear, the beverage supply is in order—it is only the food which needs to take a palatable form." Edward fetched a bottle of rum from his cabinet and poured it into two glasses.

"That is of little comfort to me on a ship, to know the captain will be in his cups the entire voyage."

"It is not as bad as that, but you will be begging me for a drink before the week's end," Edward assured him, and handed him his cup. "I bribe the crew with their daily rations. I predict you shall beg, too."

Charles held out his hand to shake on it.

"I will also shake on being able to lure your sister from her hellish box on water."

"You have a deal. But I will not assist you in that endeavour."

"I would be disappointed if you did," he remarked with a mischievous grin. "If your sister is so shy, how in the world did Gardiner manage to marry her? He scarcely said ten words the entire first term at Eton."

"Excellent observation," Charles said. "I have wondered many times myself. However, he was often at home with me during holidays."

"The sly fox," Edward said appreciatively as he sipped his drink. He leaned against the wall with one boot propped up on a trunk.

"Perhaps you can draw that information from Anjou yourself, since you think yourself clever enough to draw her out," Charles suggested.

"I will be fortunate if she does not butcher me to pieces before the journey is over."

"You and I both!"

"Did your other sisters grow up to be as beautiful?"

"Aye. They are identical, and it is a curse! However, the two lively ones are left to my parents to deal with."

"How do you mean to deal with the one you have?"

"I mean to do my best to help her find Gardiner. After the War Office declared him dead, my father sent private investigators to search for him, but they have come up with nothing."

"And your sister believes she can do better than they?" Harris queried with a doubtful raise of the eyebrow.

"She thinks there is a chance he might have been injured and be unrecognisable."

"I suppose it is a possibility, even if remote," Harris conceded as he swirled his drink.

"We know he sailed over on the same ship as Easton."

"The war was almost ended by that point," Edward remarked.

"Yes, Easton was shot during the burning of Washington City, and had no knowledge of Gardiner afterwards."

"So you will be able to minimise the search to the region between Baltimore and Alexandria? There were a few casualties at the end, on the eastern coast. Is it known when he went missing?"

"Only that it was after Washington. That is why we have chosen to stay at River's Bend."

"River's Bend is a lovely place, especially now it has been rebuilt. Maybe one day…"

"Thinking of giving up the high seas?" Charles enquired.

"It was initially a means to an end. I have some capable mates I could turn day-to-day operations over to. My mother's letters are constantly hounding me to settle down."

Charles groaned in sympathy. "Yours and mine both. We are only just past thirty years!"

"I cannot imagine dropping anchor permanently. I fear the tedium of a constant life."

"I have not managed to do so myself. I suppose when this business is finished I will need to find a useful diversion."

"You certainly have one now," Edward pointed out.

"Indeed. Hopefully we will do more than have a lovely holiday. I am afraid she will be disappointed somehow."

"There is little chance for a good outcome, Charles. If Aidan was his normal self he would have been home to her long ago."

"Yes," Charles replied with a long face. "I know that he will either not be found, or be severely changed. The Aidan we knew would never willingly abandon Anjou."

"Who would?" Edward said quietly while he stared out of the small window of the cabin.

Chapter Three

Anjou was not feeling very well this morning. She had indeed been troubled by the seasickness during the first few days, though it had improved as Elly had said it would. But the previous night had been rough; no sooner had she fallen asleep than her body had been thrust against the side of her cabin. Hannah, too, had been swaying back and forth in her hammock, and there was constant noise—it seemed the sailors' work never ended. There was always the bellowing of orders and repetition by the crew, followed by loud chanting back and forth. She had quickly learned to brace herself after hearing 'Mainsail haul', for it meant the ship would soon turn, causing her to list and lurch.

Anjou had desperately wished she could have run from the cabin to see why they were tossing and bouncing. But it would not have lessened her terror, and she would have likely realised her worst fear of ending up as food for the creatures of the deep. She had learned from Hannah that their cabin was directly adjacent to the Captain's—where her brother also stayed—and she pulled her cover over her head instead of going above to see what was happening.

Once the storm had passed, she had drifted into a fitful sleep, one where she had dreamed about Aidan. Buildings and other soldiers surrounded him; there was shouting and smoke. She could see someone lifting a gun over his head…and in that moment she awoke.

Four days of staying in the cabin and eating nothing but gruel was beginning to wear upon her. She prayed that the winds would be favourable and the voyage as swift as possible! She had researched every possible ship she could take and had selected this schooner for its repute as one of the fastest and its ability to manoeuvre against the wind. However, they were still at the mercy of the weather. She was determined to maintain control, yet she needed to see the sky and breathe some fresh air soon. Would the infuriating Captain never sleep? He was becoming more of an ogre in her mind as the days progressed.

Charles visited several times each day to play cards, and it helped alleviate some of the boredom. But he had not been able to find a time when Captain Harris was asleep and she awake. It was almost as if the Captain knew her intentions and was staying awake deliberately. She knew it was ludicrous to think such things, but perhaps this small wooden box with no fresh air or daylight was beginning to affect her.

She tossed over a spoonful of gruel in her bowl, thinking, *even I could cook better than this*. Nevertheless, whilst never having taken an ocean-wide voyage, she realised there might be nothing else available to cook.

She longed for some runny eggs, savoury bacon, and fresh warm scones just from the oven. She slammed the spoon into the bowl—she must stop torturing herself. It brought to mind another memory of Aidan—she had met him that next morning long ago secretly, and he had not only taught her to fish but how to cook it.

"Now take the fish by the gills so it doesn't move about and slip it from the hook."

She stared at him blankly.

"Go on," he urged.

She reached out and touched the fish with a shaking finger and it wrangled back and forth, causing her to jump.

Aidan chuckled. "I am not going to do it for you this time."

Anjou wrinkled her face in frustration and grabbed the fish and took it off the hook in the way Aidan had shown her. She tossed it to the ground as fast as she could with disgust, however.

"That is a start," he said with amusement. "Now you have to cook it."

He took one of the fishes he had caught and began to show her how to prepare it. He handed her a knife and she proceeded to follow his example, even though her stomach was churning. She was determined to show him she could manage it. She did not want him to think her a coward.

He placed the prepared fish in a pan and began to arrange some sticks he had gathered for a fire. He pulled a flint and steel from a small pouch and lit the wood. There was a small puff of blue smoke, followed by tiny orange flames licking at the tinder.

"Where did you learn to do all of this?" she asked.

"My grandfather. He was a soldier and thought all men should know how to fend for themselves."

"I suppose it would be necessary for a soldier to know."

"Perhaps even for a soldier's wife," he said with a sheepish grin.

How gentle and kind Aidan was. Nothing like that brute of a man Captain Harris! But, in total, she had spent less than a fortnight with Aidan. How well had she truly known the man she had married? How much of what she felt for him was a product of her own longing and imagination?

She had pined for him with her young heart, she had feared for him, and she had mourned and grieved for him, yet she scarcely knew him. Would she even recognise him today?

She had clung desperately to her memories of them as children—few though they were, and she could no longer remember his face or his smell without his picture or his four letters.

How naïve they had been! She had now observed society from a distance for over four years, and she realised she had known nothing at all when they had married. However, if they'd had opportunity to know one another on a daily basis, she had little doubt they would have persevered.

But how would it be if she found him? Had he deliberately chosen not to return to her? Something in her heart told her he was not dead, which she feared almost more than if he were.

Stop this, she chastised herself. You cannot poison your mind against him. *However*, her mind argued, *you also cannot be unprepared for whatever situation arises*. What if he is disfigured or crippled? He would not want her to see him like that. Maybe she was making a mistake, but it would not be right. No, she must have peace in her heart. There could be no turning back now—she was already in the middle of the ocean.

Anjou was glad no one knew she had married. She did not think many would understand that she had already spent her entire youth on tears and grief, should she not wear the willow for Aidan upon her return. It had been a battle of guilt and anguish, resisting the attentions of charming suitors, while all the time wondering if it were in vain. Her parents had allowed the marriage when she had forced their hands, but they had been quick to urge her to carry on with her life when the War Office had declared him killed in action; especially after three years had passed with no reports of him having been taken prisoner.

It still did not seem real. In some ways it felt as though it were a fairy tale she had daydreamed. In other ways it seemed as though she was still waiting for him to come home to her.

~*~

"She is a stubborn one. I will have to sleep eventually," Edward said to no one in particular.

"Who is stubborn?" Charles prompted, although he knew the answer.

"We've had slop for every meal. At this rate, we will all have scurvy before the journey's end."

"Then you should ask my sister to help, though I have no idea how she would fare."

"Not yet."

"You are content to eat slop?"

"Long enough to watch you grovel."

Charles laughed. "This reminds me of our first week at school. No one would snitch so we all ate gruel for a week. They dared not feed us any more for fear our parents would hear of it."

"It was funny, then," Edward said fondly. "I need real food now."

"I cannot even recall what the prank was…" Charles remarked.

"It was Gardiner. He strung Belcher's drawers out on the line after Belcher bullied him about a paper he refused to write for him. Now here I am again, eating gruel for a week because of him."

"Sorry, old fellow, you cannot blame this one on him. This is your pure stubbornness."

Edward grunted.

"You are relying quite a lot on the fact that Anjou can cook. What if she burns the kitchen down?"

"She can cook. I just know."

"Do as you please. I hope you come up with a plan before all the stores go to waste."

"So do I."

"Why do you not rest? You look haggard."

"I feel haggard. I suppose I will rest for a bit. The seas are calm enough for now."

~*~

Anjou heard a tap on the cabin door.

"Anj? Wake up!" Charles whispered loudly from the other side of the panel.

"What is it, Charles?" she asked as she opened the door as she hastily pulled on her dressing gown.

"He is finally sleeping. Hurry."

She grabbed her cloak and hurried after him up the companionway to emerge through the hatch on to the deck. She inhaled as deeply as she could of the fresh air and pointed her face towards the clear sky and shining sun.

"This is pathetic," Charles said as he watched her.

"Perhaps. It is part self-preservation. It would be more tolerable if there were better food."

"Agreed. One ceases to wonder why mutiny occurs," he remarked dryly.

"Do you think the ogre is hiding the good food from us?"

"I-I..." Charles stuttered.

"We should go and look while he is sleeping," she said with a mischievous grin.

"Anjou, no."

"Where is the kitchen?" she asked, ignoring his warnings.

Charles laughed.

"What amuses you?" Anjou asked. She began to look about the deck and noticed the leery looks of sailors watching her as they stood near the fo'c'sle of the ship. She ignored the stares and continued on around a large mast, stepping around ropes and hooks, towards the centre of the deck.

"There is no such thing as a kitchen on a ship."

"How would I know otherwise? Take me to the place where they prepare food and store it."

Charles gave a slight grin and indicated with his head for her to follow. The ship was much more extensive than she had imagined, though the deck felt small against the backdrop of the endless sea. He led her down another ladder, some narrow passageways and into a dark area he referred to as the hold. In it, there was an incredible amount of food stored in bags and barrels and Anjou gasped in irritation.

"I cannot believe it," she exclaimed. "Why is he feeding us gruel for every meal?"

Charles shrugged. "I suppose you could ask him."

She pulled a childish face at him. "You are, as ever, the most helpful of brothers. You know I do not wish to speak to the brute."

"He has become an ogre and a brute now, eh?"

Ignoring him, she held the lantern higher. "This food will go to waste if it is not eaten! Or does he feed the crew and it is only me he feeds as a slave? Will you take me to the cook, Charles?"

He looked hesitant.

"Shall I find him myself?" she threatened.

"I will take you to the galley. I refuse to take you to the crew's quarters."

He led her back up to the tween-deck of the ship.

There was a young orderly stoking a fire in a large stove in the middle of the room and refilling a kettle over it. The remainder of the space was lined with cupboards and lipped shelves for storage.

He nervously stood at attention when he noticed his visitors.

"My name is Anjou," she said sweetly, to put the boy at ease.

"Name's Biggs, m'lady."

"Are you the cook, Biggs?" Anjou asked.

"Yes'm," he said uncertainly. "Well, no'm. Cook didn't come on this journey."

"Is gruel the only thing you know how to prepare?"

"Yes'm," he answered timidly.

Anjou threw her hands up. "Is there any fish?"

"In the sea."

"Yes, I know," she said patiently. "Do you have any fish in the stores?"

"No'm, exceptin' some herring in a barrel. We don't eat fresh fish till the meats is gone or we have the doldrums. Cap'n won't stop the ship for it. But there's plenty of meat and Cook makes it the same way he does fish."

"Could you kindly fetch me some meat, then?"

The orderly went to the hold as Anjou requested.

"What are you going to do with it?" Charles asked.

"Aidan taught me to cook fish," she stated.

"Will wonders never cease?" Charles mused.

"You need not look so surprised," she snapped.

"In my defence, ladies do not venture into the kitchen often, and I have never seen you prepare anything."

"Perhaps not, but I did occasionally sit and watch Cook, so maybe I can draw from recollection. Besides, unless you wish to eat gruel for several more weeks, I must attempt it."

"I suppose there is no harm in trying."

The orderly returned with a barrel in his arms and a sack slung over his back. Inside the barrel was a large side of mutton and the bag held potatoes and carrots. He pried open the lid and emptied the contents on the table.

"That looks nothing like fish," Anjou said, staring at the pile of food.

"I went to fetch the meat, and remembered Cook would make potatoes and carrots with it when we 'ave 'em," he said proudly.

Anjou tried not to wrinkle her face in disgust at the raw meat sitting on the table in front of her. The fish had been foul enough, but this was worse.

"I remember our cook used to put carrots and potatoes in a pot with mutton for the servants, Anjou. Perhaps you could put this in the pot together and set it on the stove?" Charles suggested.

"Yes, thank you, I believe I gathered as much," she said to her brother. "Why do you not keep watch for our beloved Captain so I can be out of sight when he awakens?"

"You mean you wish to hide? Are you not going to tell him you are cooking?"

"Of course not! I do not intend to speak to the man again, if I can help it."

"Will you let him eat the food?"

"It is his ship, after all. I am not certain I could prevent it. As long as he does not know I have done the cooking and thinks it to be the work of Biggs, here, I shall not worry my head over it."

Charles thought for a moment. "I can support that," he said with a sly grin. "But let us not be hasty; let us see how the mutton stew tastes."

"You may leave, now," she directed her brother with a quelling stare. She then watched the orderly chopping and peeling carrots and shook her head. Apparently, it was too much for him to have thought of on his own.

She picked up a knife and started peeling and chopping herself, which was much harder than it looked, until they had filled the pot with mutton and vegetables.

The orderly lifted the pot over the fire, and she sat down on a small stool, feeling exhausted. A measure of respect for Cook and her underlings stroked her mind. To think they served three meals per day at the very least!

Biggs stared at her, scratching his chin and looking confused.

"What is wrong, Biggs?" she asked.

"I think Cook would add some flavouring to the pot. But I can't remember which ones."

Anjou walked over to where he was staring at some labelled jars.

"I suppose there is little harm in adding a few. I know our cook used to season everything."

She reached over and selected three jars. She opened the lids and peered inside. She had no idea how much to put in.

"Do you know how much Cook used?"

"I don't know," he said, shrugging his shoulders.

"I guess we'll try some today and see." She poured some from each jar.

"How long does it take to cook?"

A long time," he said. "I usually stir every hour when I hear the bells until it is time to eat. The crews eat in shifts."

"That seems reasonable."

"What is that I smell?" She heard a voice booming, followed by loud boots on the deck. Anjou ducked behind a cupboard. *Why does he always sound angry?* Would he be furious with Biggs?

"Did you suddenly remember how to cook, Biggs?" The Captain asked as he leaned against the post.

"Aye, aye sir," the young sailor said as he stood at attention.

"Interesting," the Captain said as he narrowed his eyes, and Anjou hoped he would not look around the small galley too closely. She took the chance to observe him more carefully, and wished he were not so big. He was in his shirt-sleeves with no waistcoat and looked as though his muscles would burst through the fabric. She had never been around a man like this. He made most men of her acquaintance appear dainty. Her brother and her father were fit men, but not so large. He was rough in both manners and appearance, with a few days' beard, and he exuded virility—so utterly different from herself.

The Captain was moving and she pressed herself closer to the cupboard. He had crossed over to the pot and was inspecting it. If he looked up, he would see her.

"Mutton. Anything is better than another bowl of gruel at this point." He lifted a spoonful and sniffed.

"How much salt and pepper did you put in there?"

"No idea, sir."

The Captain looked sceptical. "I suppose we will see how it turns out. Thank you for trying, Biggs." He slapped the boy on the back in a friendly manner, surprising Anjou.

Maybe he just did not like women. She had heard there were men like that.

~*~

"I say I win the bet," Edward insisted as they stood talking on the

41

quarterdeck.

"Nonsense," Charles argued. "You did not convince her, she did it of her own volition."

"Perhaps, though as I recall, the terms were not so specific."

"Does it matter if you have better food to eat?"

"I am not so certain it will be better. I think she dumped half the jar of salt into the cauldron. If that stew is edible I will eat my hat."

Charles laughed. "She will be devastated if it tastes bad—almost as much as she will be if she finds out you know she is cooking."

"You think so?" Edward asked thoughtfully. "Maybe if I were to sneak in there and dilute it with something, it could be salvaged."

"Something as in bourbon?" Charles suggested. "Would I lose my wager if I have bourbon in my food?"

Edward eyed his friend. "I will ignore it on this occasion, even though you will not credit me with the matter of your sister cooking." He walked over to the chest where he kept his spirits and searched through it for a few minutes before pulling out a bottle. "This should do nicely. Is your sister still in the galley?"

"No." Charles shook his head. "I sneaked her back to her quarters."

Edward allowed his deep laugh to rumble around the small room.

"I have not had so much fun since..." his voice trailed off. "Never mind. I will go and see if I can save dinner."

He was deliberately heavy-footed as he neared the galley in case Lady Anjou was back. He had struggled to keep his composure when he had seen her hiding earlier. If she had only known her skirts were billowing over the side of the cupboard! And her hair too! He laughed out loud. Passing through the doorway, Edward frowned. No one was in the galley. Maybe Biggs had gone for a short break, but he needed to have someone to watch the stove. The most dangerous thing on a ship was fire. Biggs was a good boy, though not too sharp. He would be easy on him with his first offence.

"Now let us see how the stew tastes," he said, hoping that it was not as bad as he feared. He took the ladle and tasted a bit of the broth. He jumped and spat out. The taste was indescribable. By the amount of salt the woman had poured into the pot, she must have had no clue the meat was packed in salt to begin with! He looked about for a place to pour off some of the liquid. He found an empty bowl and spooned out as much as he could. He then poured in the wine and added some water.

"Maybe that will do the trick," he said to himself as he stirred the pot. He took another small taste from the spoon. "Not too bad," he commented to the cauldron. "There is hope yet." With a self-satisfied smile, he sneaked out of the galley with the bowl of salted stew hidden beneath a sack, in order to covertly dispose of it.

Chapter Four

Thus began the charade of Anjou sneaking into the galley every day to help with meals. Several pleasant days passed quickly spent preparing food in the kitchen. As long as she remained below the main deck, it did not prove too difficult to avoid the Captain. Word quickly spread among the crew—and they thought it a great game to play on their master. She won them over one by one, especially as her cooking skills improved, for which credit belonged to having found some receipts from the cook. She had been surprised her first stew was palatable when she realised how much seasoning she had added.

It was astonishing how one's mood could improve with a proper meal. Well, not quite proper, but it was certainly preferable to the same thing over and over again. She found herself enjoying the work—taking her mind away from her troubles and tedium of the journey. Pea soup, pickled cabbage with salted beef and shepherd's pie were not on her list of favourites, having grown up with a French mother and French chef, but it was necessary to make do with the choices available. In the hold, just below the galley, there were barrels of cured meats and fish, potatoes and barley, cabbage and peas, in addition to the flour, sugar and biscuits—lovingly referred to as 'tack' by the men. And those were only the barrels she could see! They were stacked floor to ceiling, or deck to overhead, as she frequently heard them say. The crew had to have been eating little more than slop these past days, she thought, as she surveyed the enormous barrels. Did they know all of this food was here? Could none of them cook at all? Maybe they were being worked too hard to care.

She found a receipt for rhubarb pie, which sounded heavenly. She had watched it be made in the past, so she was hopeful she could manage. She found flour, sugar, and butter, but where was the rhubarb? She went to the hold and looked around, but could find no barrels with fruit of any sort. Perhaps there were fresh supplies somewhere she did not know of. She would have to ask Biggs when he returned. She did spy a cupboard and started to walk towards it when she heard a scratching noise. Before she could turn, something ran across her feet and she screamed.

Biggs came down the companionway with his arms full of eggs and a pail of milk slopping over the sides.

"What is it, m'lady?"

She was too terrified to speak. Instead, she began to point to the corner, holding her hand against her chest as it heaved from fright.

"Did somethin' scare ye?"

She nodded.

"It was probly jus' one of the rats. Cat will catch 'em."

She picked up her skirts and ran past him up the ladder before she could find out. She made it to the galley and stopped to catch her breath. Rats? Would there also be lice and other vermin too? She began to itch as she thought about those nights when they had been fleeing the terror in France, where they were forced to endure rats, lice, and all other sorts of unpleasantness. And now, she was willingly subjecting herself to them. She shuddered. Any hope of pleasant dreams had now vanished.

"Are ye all right, m'lady?" Biggs asked as he lugged the eggs and milk up after her.

"Yes, but I do not care for rodents."

"Neither does the Cap'n. He keeps the cat to take care of 'em."

One mark against him could be forgiven, she thought, but perhaps he needed another cat.

"Are those eggs? And milk? Where did they come from?"

"Well, there be goats and chickens," Biggs said without a hint of guile. She had not known there were animals on board, but she knew where eggs and milk came from!

One of the sailors hurried down the ladder through the galley past them without a nod or hello. He had his hair in a long braid and a knitted cap on his head.

"'E's afraid to speak to you. A'feard 'e'll lose 'is ration of rum," Biggs explained as she stared after the man.

"He told you not to speak to me?"

"Not 'xactly. But 'e said it'd best be proper talk fer a lady and most don't know'd how."

She found most of the men were as timid around her as she was them, and it eased her distrust of them. They had to pass through the galley to their quarters, but they seldom said a word to her, though she could overhear them speaking to one another. They were a crude bunch, to be sure, but she could see they were making an effort to mind their belches and language when she was near—at least the parts she could understand. Most of their vernacular was foreign to her, but now she understood why they were behaving.

The Captain and Charles took their meals with the mates in the Captain's saloon, and she ate alone, despite the invitation to join them. The fewer words she exchanged with Captain Harris, the better.

She began to mix the ingredients listed on the receipt for the crust.

"Biggs, do you know where the rhubarb is to be found?"

He looked at her blankly.

"Do you know what rhubarb is? I need it for the pie."

He shook his head. "Cook never made pie."

"I have the receipt right here, so he must have," she insisted. "I need rhubarb. Perhaps the Captain keeps it in a special place?"

Fear crossed the young man's face.

"Would you please go and ask him?" She looked at him in appeal, and a much lesser man would have succumbed to her big blue eyes, let alone this gangly youth who rarely saw a woman.

Swallowing hard, Biggs nodded and walked away to do her bidding.

~*~

Edward looked down from the quarter-deck and saw Biggs standing there, looking extremely nervous. He could not remember him ever venturing up here. He must need something in the galley.

"Can I help you, Biggs?"

"Aye, sir."

"Go on, then," he said encouragingly, trying to be patient with the young lad.

"Aye, sir. Would you happen to have some rhubarb?"

"Did you say rhubarb, Biggs?"

"Aye, sir. I think so."

"What would I do with rhubarb?"

Biggs' cheeks turned red and he began to stumble over his words. Edward tried hard not to enjoy himself.

"She, I mean *I* was going to use it for a pie, sir."

"Pie? Is there a special occasion?"

This was clearly beyond the boy's comprehension and means of deception.

"I dunno, sir."

"I tell you what, Biggs. I do not have rhubarb. However, I believe there are enough apples in my cabin."

The lad stood there stupefied.

"Connors, take over the helm," Edward ordered the first mate.

"Aye, aye. Take over the helm, sir," Connors shouted in reply.

Edward led the boy to his cabin, where he found a small basket of apples still remaining. He had no idea how many apples it would take to make a pie or two, but he did not want to disappoint the lady. He handed the basket over to Biggs with a small sigh of disappointment. There had not been many from his estate this year, but his crew would be over the moon if they had apple pie for their dinner. He made a mental note to re-stock at their next stop with any fruit suitable for pie-making.

"Biggs, are the men causing any trouble in the galley?"

"No, sir. Only the rats."

"A rat in the galley?"

"In the hold, sir."

"I will see to it. And if there is any improper talk around the lady or her maid, I want to hear of it.

"Aye, aye, sir."

"Shall I help you carry the apples?" Edward asked, almost toying with the boy to see his reaction.

"N-no, sir." The boy saluted and took off with the fruit.

Edward chuckled as Biggs left. This trip had been more entertaining than any other he could recall. He had never imagined Lady Anjou would be intimidated enough by him to avoid him, nor stubborn enough to carry through with her proclamation to do so!

Even the crew had reversed their opinions about having a lady on the ship quick enough.

It seemed when the men realised Lady Anjou and her maid were earning their keep on board by cooking, and no evil had befallen them, they began to believe the women were good luck charms. There were none so superstitious or fickle as sailors, he mused.

A time or two, when Edward had gone near the galley, a wall of men had formed in front of him, all with created excuses for something he must see to on the other end of the boat, of course.

It was quite amusing, how they had changed their tune and wanted to protect Lady Anjou. He was not certain how long to let the charade continue. Perhaps as long as there was no harm. The weather had been unusually favourable, save the one rough patch, and they had travelled half-way to their destination in only fourteen days. Would she be able to continue to evade him for the remainder of the voyage? He wondered as he washed up and left his cabin. He heard the crew singing *Haul Away Joe* with their usual zest as they did every day when they swabbed the decks and hauled the rigging. Gaffney, the Bosun, was leading the shanty as he climbed the ladder to the deck.

Naow when Oi wuz a little boy an' so me mother told me,
'Way haul away, we'll haul away Joe!
That if Oi didn't kiss the gals me lips would all grow mouldy.
'Way haul away, we'll haul away Joe!
An' Oi sailed the seas for many a year not knowin' what Oi wuz missin',
Then Oi sets me sails afore the gales an' started in a-kissin'.

"Oi got a bette one fer ya!" Gaffney said merrily.

But this morning there was a new tune to Edward's ears, causing him to pause before regaining the deck, as Gaffney began bellowing:

T'ere once was a gal named An-jou
T' bonniest lass wi' eyes so blue
At first me thinks her too purty
Til she made me a smile an' adieu!

It wasn't perfectly rhythmic, but that was not the point. The song was greeted by cheers and laughter, which prompted the second verse, which left Edward speechless:

Cap'n growled when he first he see'd t' lady
And we fear'd fur our rations 'o rum
But now he just grins 'n says 'oy matey!
An' I fell from aloft t' me bum!

"More! More!" the men shouted.

She cooks an' she bakes t' feed us
An' it still be t' ol nasty split peas
Ne'r mind some burnin' or tuf-nus
It's done brought t' great man to his knees!

The men were roaring with laughter, as they stamped their feet and clapped their hands. Edward listened and he had to turn to hide his smile in case someone happened upon him. It was true; this mite of a chit was pulling at his minuscule heart. He was charmed by her graceful shyness and her quiet stubbornness. Every other ounce of his being was screaming at him to turn and run, because she should be afraid of him—probably *much* afraid of him. If his men could already see he was smitten, it was a good thing they would reach land soon.

~*~

Anjou stared at the basket of apples. She supposed it was considerate of the Captain to donate his personal fruit, even though he had not offered anything to her personally, she thought, in a burst of uncharacteristic bitterness. However, the receipt called for rhubarb, not apples, and she did not know if you could substitute one for the other. Where was Hannah? She might know. Hannah was not afraid of the men, and she preferred being on deck in the fresh air to being confined inside. She was supposed to be with Anjou, but she was often out flirting with one of the mates; whether the first, second, or third, Anjou could not remember.

"Biggs? Could you please ask my maid Hannah to come to the galley?"

"Aye, my lady."

As she waited for Hannah, she felt something rub up against her legs, and she was afraid to look. Did rats grow so big? Trying not to scream, she jumped back and heard a meow.

She breathed a huge sigh of relief. She glanced down to see a solid grey cat, which was looking up at her with pleading golden eyes.

"So you must be Cat," she said as she knelt down to greet it. Her hand was briefly smelled and its head then rubbed up against it. "You do not look like a vicious rat-catcher," she mused. She stood as she heard her maid coming, and the cat settled itself at her feet.

"Hannah," she asked.. "Do you know if I can substitute apples for rhubarb in a pie?"

"I don't see why not, my lady."

Anjou handed her the cooks list of ingredients. "This seems reasonable," Hannah said.

"But Monsieur would add cinnamon, miss."

"I cannot think it likely we would have cinnamon on board." She looked to Biggs, who was stirring the pot of pea soup. She decided to see for herself. She opened the cupboard where she had found the seasonings. There were not many. Nevertheless, hiding behind the salt and pepper, she did indeed find small jars of nutmeg and cinnamon.

"Well, I'll be. Do you need help rolling the dough, my lady?"

"I did not realise that dough needed to be rolled," Anjou confessed. "If you would be so kind as to show me how."

"I did spend some time in the kitchen when I was small."

"Now you mention it, I would be pleased for some help."

"Yes, my lady. If you prefer to allow me..." the maid said, looking chagrined at not having offered to help sooner.

"No, no. I am rather enjoying it, and not being shut away in the cabin."

Hannah began to work on the dough, and Anjou looked at the apples.

"You must peel them, miss."

"Of course." Why must everything be peeled? It was one of her least favourite jobs in the kitchen.

As she became lost in piles of peel, she began to reminisce again about her time with Aidan.

They had begun to sneak away to spend time together during the few visits he had made to their home when on holiday with Charles. He was always a perfect gentleman, as far as he could be since they were alone, but he was almost as shy as she was and had not dared disrespect her.

One day, they had been chasing each other through the orchards, and when they had finally stopped to rest and eat apples under one of the trees, she had noticed Aidan had grown solemn.

"Why the long face? Is something the matter?"

He plucked a few blades of grass and sat quietly for a time.

"Are you going to tell me?" she asked, growing worried.

"I will not be returning to Oxford."

"I beg your pardon. I did not mean to intrude," Anjou said, not wishing to cause offence.

"I must go into the service of His Majesty."

Anjou gasped. Her brother had also spoken of wishing to join the fight, but thus far her parents had not allowed it.

"No! I do not want you to leave," she pleaded.

Aidan leaned over and brushed her hair back and placed a soft kiss on her lips.

"I am not very good with words, Anjou, but I want to marry you one day. Will you wait for me?"

Was he meaning what she thought he was?

"How long must I wait? The time between your visits feels like an eternity already."

He smiled. "I feel the same, but I have little to offer you until I return. I cannot imagine your father would look upon my suit favourably. I do not know if I will return, and even if I do, I may not be whole."

"I wish to be your wife."

"I promise you, when the war is over and should you feel the same, I will be yours."

She shook her head. "No."

Rarely was she defiant, but when she made up her mind, she was fierce.

"We must speak to my parents now."

"Anjou. We must be reasonable. The army is no place for a lady."

"What if you never come back to me?"

"That is precisely my point. Do you wish to be a widow? What if I leave you with child?"

"I do not wish to think about life without you," she said, taking his hand and holding it to her.

"But you must, my heart."

"Then I shall cherish the time and the gift of life, if that is what I must do."

She willed him to understand. She pulled his face to hers and kissed him, pouring forth all the love her young heart could impart.

They had spoken to her parents, and she had told them Aidan was leaving, and she would marry him before he went. Although she had not denied pre-empting their vows, she had been deliberately obtuse. She had felt guilty about misleading them, but she knew no other way to gain their compliance. In exchange, she had to promise to keep the marriage secret. Her father had always been indulgent, and would likely have given in eventually. Her father had promptly found a Catholic priest willing to marry them for a substantial sum.

Of course she had not understood what she was doing to herself. She had been young and reckless, but five years ago, it had seemed the right thing to do, to a girl of seventeen with no idea of the world beyond her.

Chapter Five

Anjou kept to her resolution to stay away from the Captain. She was certain the crew had discovered her fear of him and were helping to distract him from her presence. She really did not interact with any of the men, save Biggs, as they ate in their mess, and she only had a few minutes a day on deck. But since the first day of the voyage, there had been no more lewd comments or spitting. If the weather was rough, she did not even have those few minutes' reprieve. The Captain did not leave the main deck unless the sailing was smooth on calm seas.

It was hard to believe they would reach America in the next day or two. The time had passed quickly once she had begun to work in the galley, and she had been so tired afterwards, she had slept well. She had been having more dreams about Aidan; they seemed to become more vivid as they grew nearer to Washington. She even occasionally felt strong pain during the dreams, but she could not see a face. She could only assume it was Aidan trying to speak to her, or show her what had happened. She did not know how to interpret the visions, but she supposed it was because she was growing closer to him each day. She did also know she and her sisters could feel each other's pain, and she could only pray no harm had come to them; she was seeing neither of her sisters' faces during her dreams. Perhaps she was subconsciously hoping they were bringing her closer to solving the mystery of Aidan's disappearance.

In the small cabin, she said a rosary for her sisters and then rose from her knees, as Cat encircled her ankles and then hopped up into her lap when she sat. She could hear the men playing music and dancing, as they often did in the evening if the seas were calm. Hannah would talk about dancing with the men, and to her surprise, Anjou found herself longing to join them. She frequently pulled her viola from her trunk and tried to accompany them. She had now learned every tune by heart, and she would close her eyes and pretend she was on deck with them. It made her miss her family less, as she and her sisters had spent hours and hours playing together. Her brother was quite the musician himself, though he would deny it if asked in public.

She had not spent as much time with Charles on the journey as she had thought she would. He had taken an interest in watching the Captain sail, and she had been cooking. Nothing on this journey had been as she had supposed it would be, but she had almost made it.

She forced herself to think of what would happen when they landed. The thoughts were not pleasant or comfortable. She would be compelled to speak to innumerable strangers, and would likely be required to ask questions about Aidan from house to house. She had not truly considered what would be required of her beyond that, for she had not actually imagined she would get here. Hopefully, the investigators would be able to direct her.

The music above stopped, but she still needed to play. Her mind used the time to think. She continued on into the mournful *Requiem in D Minor* by Mozart and poured her feeling into every legato. Soon she heard a violin's higher melody joining her from the adjacent cabin. Her bow paused for a moment in wonder, and then continued, overcoming her apprehension. Someone had heard her, and someone knew the music she played. Her heart began to pound as the duet felt intimate and equally passionate. Charles had not brought a violin, and she was certain it was not he. He would have joined her instead of disguising himself behind a wall. She soon stopped thinking and lost herself in the beautiful harmony, feeling tearful when it ended.

~*~

"This game has worked out rather nicely," Charles mused later in the evening, as he and his friend were readying themselves for bed.

"Indeed. Your sister is even beginning to become a decent cook. Too bad the journey is almost at an end. My men will miss her," Edward said as he poured himself a drink and smiled while Charles watched longingly.

"My sisters tend to have that effect on people," Charles remarked sympathetically. "But sailors are not typical people."

"You speak the truth," Edward said dryly. "Do you have a plan for searching for Gardiner?"

"Somewhat. I have maps and some good contacts gained from Sir Charles Abbott, along with a letter of introduction. He said the Americans are wary of the British, but are not completely unreasonable," Charles explained.

"I trade with some of the farmers, and will be happy to help if need be. I will ask around, but if the investigators have found nothing, I cannot imagine I will."

"Anjou believes it will take more than asking. She is convinced the investigators are enjoying my father's income."

"Perhaps," Edward agreed. "You will be doing a great deal of work searching. Does your sister realise this could take months, even years? This country is much vaster than England. If Gardiner does not wish to be found, he could have taken off into the wilderness. He will never be discovered if he does not want to be."

"I will speak to her again about it. I think she realises, but she feels she must try."

"Your sister is an unusual woman. Loyalty is not common amongst the fairer sex, as far as my acquaintance of it has shown."

"I am sorry to hear it," Charles said. "I may claim the opposite amongst the women I am fortunate to know."

Edward held his tankard up in acknowledgement, and then turned to stare out of the small windows in his cabin. He appeared lost in thought.

"I will be in the West Indies for a few weeks. I will return to River's Bend before departing, so leave word there if you wish to return with me. I cannot say precisely when I will be back again, but I will be returning before the winter."

"I hope to convince her to limit the search to the immediate area around Alexandria. If we have a strong clue, I will, of course, follow it."

"Does your sister believe she will be able to inspect every worker on every farm?"

"She is stubborn and has a charm about her. It is her shyness I have concern for, but she is more determined than I have ever seen her."

"I wish you both well in your quest. Gardiner was a good man."

"Aye."

They both spent the rest of the evening reminiscing about childhood antics amongst the four of them—Yardley, Gardiner, Edward, and Charles.

Charles took off his boots to lie on his bunk. "Consider staying with us at River's Bend."

"I always stay with my ship, but thank you."

"The offer stands, nonetheless. Good night."

~*~

Anjou could not help feel some sense of anticipation as she heard one of the men shout, "Land ho! All hands on deck!"

She was desperate to catch her first glimpse of America and made sure Hannah had her belongings safely ensconced in her trunk. She knew the Captain to be above deck, so she looked cautiously into the passageway and knocked on the adjacent cabin door.

"Charles? Are you in there?"

"I am," he replied, grinning as he opened the door.

"Did you hear them call 'land ho?' Does it mean what I think it means?" she asked excitedly.

"It does. We have been skirting the shore for most of the last two days and have now arrived in a bay. We go by river to Alexandria. Come, I will show you on the map." He held the door open for her and she peered in suspiciously.

"Do you think I would hide the Captain in here?" he asked with amusement.

"Perhaps."

It was the first time she had seen the cabin, which was considerably nicer and more spacious than her own. Charles had gone to a small table with a map spread across it. He was pointing out their location and where they had come from the night before. She took note, but was also quietly taking in small details about the Captain. The tidy space was elegant with its mahogany panels and white paint, decorated in a similar fashion to her father's study. There were portraits of his family she wanted to peruse but did not; there were several books, a violin, and a pipe. His scent, which she recognised from their brief encounters, filled the air. He suddenly felt more human to her after seeing his private quarters.

Charles was still pointing to places on the map and turned to the window to show her where they were. She eagerly looked and took in her first sight of America.

"How nice it is to have windows," she exclaimed.

"It is good to be the Captain," Charles agreed. "He expected you to demand a trade."

"Would he have done so?" She was astonished at the thought—it had never occurred to her.

"One can never tell with Edward. He might have insisted you sleep in here with him if you wished for this cabin." He chuckled.

"And you wonder why I think him a beast?"

"I did not say I wondered."

"This does not look so different from home," she said, noticing the tall trees lining the water.

"No, although in England, you would be greeted by chalk cliffs. And it feels much warmer here, as far as I can gather."

"How much longer do we have?"

"If we keep at our current speed, we should be there within two hours."

"Two more hours?" she cried. "I do not think I can bear one more minute!"

"It is not easy to manoeuvre the ship in smaller spaces, especially with the traffic near a port," he explained.

"I had not considered," she confessed. "I am quite eager to feel land beneath my feet again."

"As am I, though I do not look forward to our duties when we arrive."

"Nor do I, but thank you for accompanying me, dear brother. I would never have arrived here without you."

"What else are brothers for?"

"I am certain I can come up with something else should I put my mind to it," she sallied.

"Forget I asked."

Chapter Six

Anjou was not sure what she had expected, but she had not supposed she would be required to go in a small rowboat to the house. However, the dock at River's Bend was not equipped for large ships. She had seen forested hills as they had approached through the bay called the Chesapeake, and as they rode up the Potomac River, it was much the same. It was very pretty, but it was much warmer than she was accustomed to. It must be mid-summer by now, she thought, though she had lost track of the weeks whilst at sea.

Charles was helping to row, along with the Captain and some of the sailors. It was uncomfortable, watching the men work while she sat idly by, a mere dainty damsel. Chanting "heave-ho," the men hauled on the oars, their muscles bulging against their sweat-soaked shirt-sleeves. She was doing no work, and she feared her own clothing must be damp with the moist heat.

At last they came to a curve in the river, where a beautiful white manor house stood on a hill overlooking the bend in the Potomac. It was aptly named. The Captain gave the order for the crew to lift their oars and they drifted around to a small wooden jetty. Two of the sailors jumped from the boat into the waist-deep water, and pushed the vessel from the back. Captain Harris stood and guided from the front until he could put one leg to the dock to stall the craft.

He held out his hand to assist Anjou, and she tried not to shy away from it. Unfortunately, the men were unloading the trunks at the same time and caused her to lurch into him.

"Oh!" she exclaimed as she came into contact with his hard, sweaty chest. She froze out of fear, her free hand clutching his bulky arm in self-preservation. He seemed to grow amused and laughed. She felt a rumble beneath her cheek.

"Brute," she muttered under her breath.

"You will find your land legs soon enough," he said, setting her back on her feet.

She was too embarrassed to speak. Why must she be so intimidated by him?

"Lady Anjou." She realised he was addressing her, so she looked up into his light green eyes.

"Yes?"

"I wanted to thank you for all of the fine meals. My men may mutiny until old Cook comes back," he said kindly, a half smile dancing over his well-formed mouth.

She was stunned speechless. He knew? Not only that, but she had proven more ill-mannered than he in forgetting to thank him for bringing her to America.

"Yes, I knew," he said, obviously reading her thoughts.

"Why?" She had many more questions to ask, but that was the only word which escaped her lips.

"I shall allow your brother to answer."

He turned to the boat, then stopped. "I hope you find what you are looking for."

He climbed into the boat where the other sailors were waiting and grinning at her. Had they all known? They tipped their hats to her and she only just recovered in time to call "thank you" back to Captain Harris as they began to row away. She could not but feel guilty that she had misjudged him.

"Are you coming?" Charles bellowed from the cart which had been brought to retrieve them and their trunks. She took one last look at the Captain and crew as they disappeared around the bend. Turning, she then walked slowly up the dock, lost in contemplation.

"Do not tell me you are sad to see the ogre go?" her brother teased.

She contemplated her response. Was she sad to see him go? She was uncertain. He had known and he had thanked her.

"He knew."

She looked up at her brother whose blue eyes were focused on her.

"He knew what?" Charles asked cautiously.

"He thanked me for cooking."

"Yes, he knew."

"That is all I am to know? He would not explain."

"Of course he would not show me that kindness. You were afraid of him," Charles pointed out.

She could sense her brother was hiding something, so she probed for more information.

"So you allow the crew was smitten with you?" Charles corrected.

She punched him in the arm in the way she had done when they were children. But she was irritated.

"I cannot believe you did not tell me, Charles!"

"I wanted to eat!"

Angrily, she turned away from him. "I was so proud of myself."

"Come now, can you honestly tell me you would have set foot outside of your cabin had you known that he knew? I can answer for you; you would not. Besides, the crew did not know that he knew."

"So it was a game between you and Captain Harris," she stated.

"Of sorts," Charles conceded.

"You are both ogres."

"Yes, but this ogre crossed the Atlantic for you and is going to help you look for Aidan, remember? And the other ogre allowed you passage on his ship."

"Yes," she muttered. "But I would prefer it if you would allow me to be angry—no, mortified—for a few minutes."

"Very well. If it makes you feel any better, I did not make any money from the bet since you decided to cook on your own."

"I beg your pardon?" She was indignant. "You placed a bet with the Captain? You should have stopped before the last sentence!"

"I have never known when to leave well enough alone."

"I will ring Captain Harris's neck if I ever see him again. I do not care if I need a ladder to do it!" she fumed.

Anjou was too angry to speak. Charles began conversing with Abe, the elderly butler, who was driving, but she remained silent. She did not even notice her surroundings as they rolled along. Why did she feel so incapable and insignificant? She was tired of everyone being amused by her shyness. It was not as if she wanted to be such. She could manage in society, where quietness and demureness were considered virtues, where she could easily blend into the crowd or with her sisters. She could manage a few polite trivialities, and as she grew to know people the shyness dissipated. She could feel herself clamming up. She wanted to be alone. The journey had taken everything out of her, and then to find out she had been the subject of a wager and joke at the instigation of her brother and that beast of a man... Her blood was boiling, and yet she was weary.

The cart pulled in front of the plantation house. They were greeted at the door by Josie, the housekeeper, just as Lady Easton had said they would be. Josie had been Lady Easton's maid and companion before she had married Lord Easton's batman, Buffy. They now lived at River's Bend and managed the estate.

"You are very welcome, Lord Winslow and Lady Anjou! We are very pleased to have you. Lady Easton wrote to inform us you would be visiting soon, so we have been sending the cart down to the docks every time we see a boat!" The pleasant, boisterous housekeeper laughed.

"We are very pleased to meet you," Charles said, speaking for them both.

"I am certain you are tired and would probably like a warm bath," Josie said. "At least that is how I feel when I have been on a ship for weeks. I will show you to your rooms and have your trunks sent up to you."

Anjou did not feel like talking, but Josie did not seem to mind. She seemed happy to fill in the conversation for her.

"We take tea at four here, but I will have it sent to your room, if you prefer. I know you have plans for your time here, and my Buffy has been talking with your father's investigators to understand where they've been. Lord and Lady Easton said we are to be at your disposal. But I can see you are tired. I'll run yer bath for you and leave you be."

Josie led Anjou into a large apartment decorated in shades of blue and grey with white wooden furniture. It was feminine, and tastefully simple. It fitted in with what Anjou knew of Lady Easton. She could hear the water being poured into the bath in the next room. The house had recently been rebuilt after it had been burned down in the not-so-distant war between Britain and America—the war Aidan had been sent to and not returned from. The reason she was here.

Hannah helped her from her dress and she sank into the deep tub of hot water. Reality began to sink in as she took in the strange surroundings. She no longer had her sisters to hide behind. Sailing to America was no longer a distant dream. It was no longer a figment of her imagination or her inner conscience telling her to go. She was here. She began to shake with fear. This was real.

~*~

Charles paced the braided rug in the study, which had been the domain of Sir Charles Abbott several years before, when he had served as minister to the Crown. He was thinking while he listened to Lord Easton's steward, Buffy, and the investigator his father had hired to search for Gardiner.

"So, you are telling me you have been to every house, plantation, and business within a thirty-mile radius?" Charles asked.

"Yes, sir," replied the investigator named Scott.

Buffy rolled out a map and put weights on the edges of it. He began to point to places marked upon it, starting from the areas around River's Bend, and then covering several miles outward from the river.

"I have personally been to Custis House, Colross, Hollin Hall, Mount Eagle, Mount Vernon, Huntley House, Gunston Hall, and the Belvoir and the Belmont plantations. I spoke to the owners and stewards I know there myself. None of them have taken in any British soldiers, or anyone fitting Gardiner's description," Buffy said.

"We have scoured the north side into Maryland, as well," Scott added as he joined them in looking over the map. "We do not have the connections there we do here in Virginia, but everyone we spoke to was emphatic they knew of no one who could be him. We even went out into the fields and looked at each place. If he is there, he is hiding and does not want to be found."

Charles sighed.

"There was one soldier who had been taken as a prisoner of war, but he was not Gardiner."

"And it has been years since it happened. I was there the night of the fire, but I did not see him afterwards, since I was seeing to Lord Easton's wounds," Buffy said. "I remember he was standing nearby when Easton was confronting Colonel Knott about his orders to burn everything in sight."

"Let us hope Colonel Knott did not punish him as he did Easton."

"I can write to my father to see if Colonel Knott may be questioned in prison. I do not expect cooperation from that corner, however."

"Should we expand our search?" Scott asked.

"The trail has gone cold by now. You could look for the rest of your lives in this country alone," Charles answered.

"We are at your disposal."

Charles sat in the chair at the desk and put his hands on his temples, thinking and looking at the map.

"Have you looked at hospitals? Spoken to physicians? Are there homes for the wounded?"

"It has been five years, my lord. We have tried, but memories of one particular wounded man are impossible to find," Scott said.

"But surely a British uniform would have stood out?"

"Precisely, my lord. There is nothing. We have had no prospects in these years of searching, and we only began after the British War Office had declared him dead. We have sent letters to every landowner in every area where British soldiers were stationed after he was last seen, with no favourable responses."

"He could be anywhere by now," Charles said despairingly. "Or he could have been killed and fallen in the river."

"What does your sister need to reassure herself?" Buffy asked.

"I wish I knew. Perhaps if I take her to speak to the plantation owners around us, she will grow weary and see the improbability herself."

"I will arrange for that," Buffy remarked.

"And if she is not satisfied?" Scott asked.

"Then we shall search until she is," Charles replied.

"Yes, sir."

Charles remained for some time in the study trying to assimilate all he had heard from Buffy and Scott. He knew searching for Gardiner was an exercise in futility. He had suspected as much before they had sailed; after reading the reports from Scott, he was now certain. However, he loved his sister and would try his best to help her. He was tired and his mind was full, but he could not seem to settle his thoughts. He took a small sip of whisky from the cabinet in the study, but after a month without any spirits, he could drink little of it.

"Perhaps a book?" He glanced over the bookshelves, mostly lined with books on history and philosophy. He suspected there had to be more of a light-hearted selection somewhere in the house. He went into the hallway and looked about for a library. He knew the doorway across the hall was the dining room, and so he tried the room next to the study.

"Success," he declared as he lifted his taper around the room.

"I beg your pardon," he said as he noticed a small woman reading on one of the sofas. He lifted his taper to see her face.

"Lady Abernathy?"

"Yes, Lord Winslow, it is I, but please do not call me that name again. I believe we can dispense with formalities." Her stark blue eyes looked at him with sadness; they had lost their old glow.

She was still a beautiful woman as she sat in her wrapper, with her golden hair down and a book in her lap, though undoubtedly more mature and experienced than she had been some ten years before. The stories of her husband's depravity must have taken their toll.

"It has been many years, Sarah."

"Indeed it has. Many unkind years."

"I am very sorry for it," he said tenderly.

She nodded. "I will not pretend you do not know what happened to my husband."

"And I will not trouble you to speak on it, but I am willing to listen should you need to. Do you now live here?" he asked.

"I do not know," she said softly. "I have been here several months. I thought removing myself would ease the pain, but I miss my children."

"Did the boys go back to school?"

"Yes, it was their wish. I could not return to that awful house. I beg your pardon, Charles. This is none of your concern."

"Nonsense. We were friends once."

"Yes, friends. I had almost forgotten what it was like to have friends."

Charles had wished for more, but he had been a silly youth still sowing his oats. He had been hurt by her dismissal and had turned away from courting. She had only had eyes for Abernathy. He had instead joined the fight against Napoleon to nurse his broken heart.

"How long do you stay in America?" she asked.

"We are searching for someone. A lost cause, I fear."

"Lieutenant Gardiner? Josie told me."

"Yes."

"A sad story. I hope your sister may find peace."

"And you too, Sarah. Maybe it is time to consider returning to England? My sister and I would welcome your company on our return."

She looked pensive for a moment. "I shall think on it. Thank you."

Chapter Seven

After her bath, Anjou fell asleep and slept through to the next morning. She was mentally and physically exhausted after the journey. This surprised and frustrated her because she wanted to begin her search immediately.

Once dressed, she went searching for Charles, whom she found in the study looking at a map and making lists. At the centre of the panelled room was a large mahogany desk, which faced two leather armchairs.

"Good morning, Charles."

"Good morning, sister. I trust you are now rested?" he asked. There was a mischievous twinkle in his eye.

"I am not convinced of that, although I certainly stayed in bed long enough. My sleep was disturbed by dreams of finding Aidan."

"Please tell me you had a premonition."

"Is the news so bad?"

"I met with one of the investigators and Lord Easton's steward for some time last evening. It appears they have been very thorough. I have been making a list of where they have already searched and the landowners to whom they have spoken."

She walked over to the desk and stood behind his chair. Peering over his shoulder at the map, she then looked at his list. She read quietly for some time.

"How far have they searched?" she finally asked.

"This is the last place he was seen by Easton and his batman, Buffy, who is now steward here." He pointed to Washington. "The investigators have searched an area spanning thirty miles from there in all directions. After we sent word we were coming, Buffy took it upon himself to speak to all the landowners in this area he knows personally."

Anjou nodded, trying to take in all of the information.

Charles told her what Buffy had said about Colonel Knott, and that he had posted a letter to their father that morning to see if the man could be questioned in prison; Colonel Knott had tried to kill Lord Easton on the night the British had burned Washington.

"Do you think there is a chance Aidan saw what happened and was killed by Knott?"

"It is possible. Although I still would have thought his body would have been found."

"I wish we had known to try to speak with him before we sailed," she complained.

"Indeed. However, we are here and must do what we may. I am at your service, sister. What would you like to do?"

"What do you advise, Charles?"

"I have to admit, it appears a thorough search has been made. If Aidan lives, he must not wish to be found."

He reached out and touched her arm as he said the hurtful words.

"I know it is possible," she whispered. "If only I could feel at peace. There is something inside me which will not let him go." She pointed to her heart as she said the words, where there was still a hole waiting to be filled.

Charles nodded. "Very well. Where shall we begin?"

"Do you think Buffy would take us to the last place he saw Aidan? Maybe I will feel something. Maybe something in my dreams will make sense."

"I do not think there is harm in trying. I will speak to Buffy and ask for the carriage to be sent around after you have partaken of breakfast. I believe the sighting was near the minister's residence, should you care to pay a call."

"We are not here for social reasons, Charles," she reminded him.

"Lady Easton's father, Sir Charles Abbott, was the British Minister at the time. Easton said he was trying to reach the residence when he was shot in the back. If you are attempting to piece together what happened to Aidan, I would suggest also going there. You may find more people with knowledge—people who might speak to us and not a hired investigator."

"Forgive me, I had not thought of it."

"And that is why your favourite brother accompanied you," he teased. "Go and break your fast, and I will arrange everything."

Two hours later they set out in a carriage for the capital of America. It was not many miles from River's Bend, and they had to cross a bridge over the Potomac River to reach it. It was another hot, humid and sunny day there. Anjou was surprised at the bustling city, which was vastly different from the countryside they had experienced across the river.

"Here we are," Buffy said as they pulled up in front of a large, imposing stone house at the corner of a wide street. "Where would you like to begin, my lady?"

Anjou looked around to take in her surroundings. "The very last place you saw him," she answered.

"Yes, my lady." Buffy directed the driver to take them further. "This is where I found Lord Easton," he said quietly, pointing to the street in front of the British Minister's residence.

"He almost made it," Charles noted.

"Yes," Buffy agreed.

They continued past several streets to a great lawn, across which the President's House sat in the distance, and stopped. "This is where we were gathered. Colonel Knott was commanding everyone to burn the city. "My lord Easton confronted him here. Lieutenant Gardiner was standing about here and watching the confrontation with great interest."

"What happened next?" she asked hopefully.

"The regiments separated, and the city began to go up in flames. Lord Easton hurried toward the Minister's residence to speak with General Ross."

"And you followed Lord Easton?"

"Not at first," Buffy said. "I wish I had. I did not notice what he was doing to begin with."

She nodded. "May I sit here a moment?"

"Of course."

She found a bench under a tree in the square and looked around. There were no visible signs of that terrible night. The sky was clear, homes and businesses had been rebuilt, and the President's House stood unmarred in white majesty, surrounded by trees and gardens. She sat and closed her eyes and tried to visualise what had taken place. Was this the location she had seen in her dreams? She tried to imagine thousands of soldiers standing where she was, people shouting, buildings on fire, and the air thick with smoke. But she could not picture Aidan.

At last she gave up.

"Let us walk the path you took," she suggested.

"I went with the regiment in this direction, towards the President's House," Buffy said, pointing. "It was not until I had begun to search for Lord Easton and did not see him that I realised where he was going and followed. I was on foot, not on horseback, so it took me some time to catch up with him."

"It is some distance to the residence," Charles noted.

"Aye." Buffy paused and sat thinking for a moment.

"Have you thought of something?" Anjou asked.

"I am not sure," he said cautiously. "I do not wish to raise your hopes, but I do remember someone shouting at me from behind as I ran. He was an officer, but I cannot be certain it was Lieutenant Gardiner."

They all sat quietly. If that had been the case, Aidan could have seen what happened to Lord Easton.

"Did the shouting follow you the entire way?"

"I cannot say. When I saw Knott shoot my lord, I could think of nothing but saving him."

"I understand. Will you take us in the direction in which you walked?"

They began to head north, and turned down a busy thoroughfare named Connecticut, which was teeming with carriages and vendors selling their wares—much as it would be in London. It was some distance, and they walked past the President's House, townhouses and businesses, the humid air fragrant with jasmine and the streets bright with summer blooms of azaleas and hydrangeas. As they grew near to the Minister's residence, Buffy stopped.

"This is where I was standing when I realised what was happening."

"Describe everything to me," Anjou requested.

He gave her a questioning look.

"Please," she pleaded. "I need to know."

He hesitated but complied. "I had been running to catch up, when I heard a shot. It was a battle, true, but this is not where the fighting and burning was, so it caught my attention. I began to hurry and I feared the worst when I saw Colonel Knott standing over Lord Easton's body, holding a gun."

Something drew Anjou to walk a little further and cross the street to where a row of brick houses ended. She stopped and closed her eyes. She could feel something, like a strong sensation of pain. Had he been here? Had he been hurt? She tried to see more from the vision, but she could not conjure up Aidan's face.

"What is it, Anj?" Charles asked. He had crossed the street to join her.

"I don't know. I feel something, but I do not know what it means," she exclaimed in frustration.

"I am sorry," he said, putting his arm around her. "Shall we go into the house and see if you feel anything there?"

"I suppose we should," she answered, though she did not particularly wish to leave when she finally felt she had found a piece of the puzzle.

She did not do any talking while inside the residence. Charles handled everything. The Minister and his wife were not in, but Charles spoke to his secretary.

"Yes, we are aware of Lieutenant Gardiner's status…yes, we realise his body was never found…unfortunately, we have been instructed not to devote any more effort to finding him. Of course, if any new information comes to light, we will reconsider…"

Anjou stopped listening. She had heard it all before. She would no doubt think the same in their situation. If she could stop feeling Aidan was alive, she thought she could let him rest in peace. She shook her head. Most people would think her a lunatic if she explained the odd visions she was subject to. She wanted to leave. She felt nothing of Aidan inside here. Capturing Charles's attention, she gestured towards the door. He gave her the slightest of nods to show he understood.

Anjou escaped past the butler, who held the door open for her, and walked back to the place where she had felt something. She allowed herself to be drawn by the sensation, which carried her past her original starting point and into an empty carriageway between two houses. The sensation was very strong. She still could not see Aidan's face, but she could picture a soldier being hit over the head, as she had in her dreams. What could it mean? Was he dead or alive?

Anjou stood there, pondering the possibilities, until Charles and Buffy joined her.

"I thought we would never find you," he chastised. "You should not run away without telling me."

"Forgive me. I did not intend to."

"Did you find something?" he asked.

She gave a slight shrug of one shoulder and looked sideways at Buffy. She was afraid to speak of her visions in front of a relative stranger.

"You may confide in him," Charles encouraged.

"I believe he was hit over the head here."

"You are certain?" Charles asked. Doubt vibrated through his voice.

"No, I cannot see his face in my dreams. But I feel it."

"But you cannot see if he lives or dies." It was not a question.

"No," she whispered.

Charles sighed. "We must go with your instincts, because we have nothing else. We have had no help from our government and no one who remembers seeing him."

"What did Colonel Knott do after he shot Lord Easton? Where did he go? If he had wanted to dispose of Aidan, what could he have done?"

"I would have thrown him across my horse and dumped him into the river," Charles said.

Buffy nodded agreement.

"Take me in the direction he might have gone."

"How would we know? The river surrounds much of this city," Charles explained.

"I would hazard a guess he would take the fastest route, if he was trying to dispose of a victim," she snapped.

"Due south or east. But the fighting was to the south, so he would have been less likely to stand out amongst it all. He might even have appeared to be trying to save a fellow soldier, if he was seen."

"Let us head south," she ordered.

They went in that direction, but the sensation was gone. Anjou stood on an embankment overlooking the river and wondered if he had met his end there. If so, why did it feel as if he were haunting her?

"Anything?"

"Nothing. Let us go."

"Do you want to try going east?" he asked.

"No, thank you," she replied and walked towards the carriage. Without looking at either of the two men, she climbed in, and sitting in the forward seat, watched the river pass by as they rode back to the plantation. She did not say a word as she fought back tears, trying to come to terms with Aidan's likely demise, and why she could not rid herself of his ghost.

~*~

Anjou took a walk around the gardens after they arrived back at the house. She was bitterly disappointed, and felt as though she had missed something Aidan had been trying to contact her earlier, though no matter how hard she had tried, his message had escaped her. She inhaled the fresh scent of pine and the fragrant lilacs about her, but nothing brought back the sensations she had experienced in Washington. She grew closer to the bend near the river and noticed someone sitting in a swing.

"Lady Abernathy?" Anjou asked when she saw the woman, who favoured Lady Easton, though she was a little older and appeared more fragile somehow. Her eyes looked tired and had a sadness about them.

"Please call me Sarah," she answered. "You are Lady Anjou?"

"I am. I hope we do not intrude."

"Not at all. My sister wrote to me of your visit. Welcome to Virginia," she replied softly, "though I have seen little myself. I do not go out."

"Please accept my condolences," Anjou said, and swatted at an insect which was biting her arm. Sarah flinched. "I am sorry, I did not mean to frighten you."

"It was just unexpected. I should not be so nervous," Sarah said dismissively.

"Did Lady Easton also tell you why I am here?" Anjou asked cautiously, despite the fact Sarah was bound to find out sooner or later.

"She said you are searching for someone," Sarah replied quietly.

"Yes, a family member who went missing during the war," Anjou explained.

Sarah gazed into her eyes for the first time, her expression full of empathy. "I hope you find what you are looking for."

Chapter Eight

Charles had been for a ride to clear his head, and think through how best to deal with his sister and how he could lead her to accept Aidan's death. He was walking back from the stables towards the house when he spied Sarah sitting on a swing, staring blankly into the distance. He could not imagine what she must have undergone while married to Abernathy, nor the humiliation she had endured. She did, in fact, seem a shell of her former self. She had once been vibrant and full of life, much like her sister Elly, yet more refined due to the differences in their upbringings. Now she seemed distant. He was concerned for her, especially living here alone. She seemed to care only for her children, yet she was an ocean away from them. Charles could not help but think she must be persuaded to return to England. He had seen soldiers with a similar look of despondence in their eyes. If they could not be convinced of their worth they continued downward—some even ended their own lives. He himself had suffered with the dismals after the war, and it was not a pleasant sensation.

"Good afternoon, Sarah. How do you do, today?"

"I do very little. It is a queer thing. I can find myself sitting in the porch swing for hours without realising it, yet I have no care to do anything about it."

"It is natural to be blue-devilled after you lose someone you cared about."

"Please do not say so."

"My apologies. I did not intend to offend you."

"I know it. But you see, I do not mourn him. I hated him."

"I can hardly blame you."

"You see why I did not wish to be in England? I refuse to play the grieving widow, as if my husband were a martyred saint."

"I do not think you need trouble yourself over it. It will soon be one year. I would expect you may safely return without fear of criticism."

"Perhaps. I have endured much for my children, and I thought it would be better for them if I left."

"But now you long to see them. I imagine they feel the same."

"I hope so, Charles. I hope they remember more of me than of the circumstances of my leaving. I can still hear Johnny's screams echoing in my head when he saw what his father was capable of."

"Sarah," Charles whispered as he feared Abernathy's depravity had been much worse than he had imagined. What had the man done to her?

"I speak too freely," she said, turning her face away.

"No." He could sense her withdrawal. "Would you care to walk with me?"

"I suppose so," she said indecisively. She was thin and somewhat pale, but it still suited her. Someone who had not known her before would not have recognised the difference, but Sarah had always had a radiance about her, an inner glow. It was gone now.

"Tell me about your children," he said, deciding upon the only topic which seemed to interest her.

"George is eight. He is a pleasant child; he loves to be with his friends. He writes to me often."

"That is something, indeed. I remember my days at Eton. I was horrid at writing my letters home."

"Johnny is nine. He is more solemn and emotional. He was very afraid for me."

"I imagine he misses you."

"Yes," she whispered. "He took the teasing about his father very ill."

"I imagine it is difficult for one so young, but he has George with him," Charles reasoned in a soothing tone.

"Yes, that is what I decided. My father and brother visit them often. They are not too far distant and of course the boys go there during the holidays."

"If you left soon, you could be there by Michaelmas."

"Perhaps so. I lost track of time," she confessed.

"It is only natural, Sarah."

"Is it? I wonder. What will it be like if I go back?" She looked down.

"I cannot answer that. I can tell you your sons will be delighted to see you, and the rest of your family will welcome you with open arms, I can assure you."

"Yes. I apologise for my conversation or lack, thereof. I have done little talking the past nine months."

"There is no need to apologise, Sarah."

"What an unnatural mother you must think me."

"I think nothing of the sort!" Charles protested.

"People judge. They believe everything must be the woman's fault when a marriage goes wrong. I grew up with a perfect example of a father, and expected all men would be as he was."

"You could not know. You cannot blame yourself."

"It is easy to tell oneself, but another thing to live with it."

"What did he do to you, Sarah?"

Tears filled her eyes and she looked away.

"I regret I asked. Forgive me, I only wish to help you."

"I know," she whispered. "I do not want to need help. I thought if I stayed away I would be able to forget. Everyone keeps telling me time heals all wounds. But I do not think it can."

"No, I do not believe every wound can be healed. But I do believe we can learn to deal with them and thence to live again," he said gently.

"I only wish I knew how."

"I think the answers are different for everyone. But promise me, Sarah, you will not give up trying."

She nodded.

~*~

Anjou had not considered she would be a novelty to some—a real lady in the latest modes from England. There were those who considered themselves high society and easily forgave any tensions between Americans and the British; then there were those with British roots who welcomed her with open arms, happy for any news from home. There were others who openly shunned them; most likely those who had suffered losses at the hands of the British. Nevertheless, it was not what Anjou had expected, and the attention was not at all what she wanted. She tried her hardest to act like her sisters, but she was who she was. The other drawback to asking questions about Aidan was the greater likelihood word would spread regarding her search for him. Thus far, Charles had said they were looking on behalf of the family, which was true.

After an afternoon with Lord Fairfax and his son at their Belvoir home, she was becoming discouraged. They had visited all the plantations in Virginia bordering the river. No more information had been turned up, only more doubt.

In the past twenty days, they had searched tirelessly; almost as long as they had been on the ship to America. For a moment, she longed to be back in England, but then her mind turned to the return trip and the ship's captain. Maybe there was another way home.

On the ride back from Belvoir, she saw a man working in a field as they rode along the narrow road back to River's Bend.

"Stop!" she cried, tapping on the roof of the carriage.

"What is it?" Charles asked in confusion.

She did not stop to answer. She leapt from the carriage and ran out to the man, convinced he was Aidan. It was just like one of her dreams. She felt as though she had been in this exact moment before.

When the man turned, he looked at her in dismay. Her chest was heaving up and down from running and the rush of hope. "You are not Aidan," she whispered, completely broken-hearted.

"I'm sorry, miss, no. The name's Jacobs." He took off his hat on the words.

She could barely mutter, "I beg your pardon," before turning and running away.

Charles was standing nearby, waiting for her. He spread his arms wide, and walking into that safe haven, she began to sob uncontrollably as he wrapped his arms around her.

"Je suis vraiment désolé," Charles whispered in her ear over and over until the sobs slowed. Then he led her slowly back through the field and into the carriage.

He held her until they arrived back at the house. He handed her down from the carriage, but instead of going inside, she began to walk the other direction.

"Anjou?" Charles called to her.

"I need to think."

"Shall I join you?"

"I think I would prefer some time alone."

"I understand. Do not become lost."

Anjou could muster no more than a quelling look. She was not in the mood to be teased. She walked for some time, taking the path to the river, but did not know why her feet led her there. Perhaps it was a sign telling her it was time to leave. She sat on the post at the edge of the dock. There was something about watching water which was conducive to reflection. A wry laugh escaped her in spite of her sombre mood. It was hard to believe she could think such a thing, she who had been deathly afraid of water little more than one month past.

She was disappointed in herself for giving up—for letting Aidan down—but was it finally time to accept he had gone? Could she? Would he allow it?

"Aidan, if you are not here any more, you must let me be. I cannot bear the burden any longer."

There was nothing at all to indicate he had survived. If he was alive, he would have tried to come back to her. She knew it.

"I must let you go."

Perhaps the problem had been within her all along. Perhaps she had needed to close the door on that part of her life by coming here to see for herself. She no longer felt she was the same person she had been when she had left England. She had been married these five years past, but had not had to mature as a wife, not with her family there to make all the decisions. It was hard enough to see your mate leave for war, but it had been even harder to be unable to mourn openly. She would have to finish grieving now, she told herself. How did one go about ending one's period of mourning? Acknowledging it was the first part of the process, she supposed. The admission brought tears to her eyes, but she brushed them away. For those brief moments this afternoon, she had truly thought she had found him. The stark realisation of looking into the eyes of a stranger, and the ridiculous scene she had made, struck her to the core. It was time to bury her childish fantasies.

"Aidan, I hope you can understand." She choked on her words. "I don't know what else to do or where to look. I hope your soul has found rest, and you can forgive me."

She slipped the small band from her locket and turned it over in her hand several times while the tears flowed. She brought it to her lips for one last kiss and tossed it into the river.

"Goodbye, Aidan," she whispered into the breeze.

She turned and ran as hard as she could until she felt numb.

~*~

"Lord Winslow," Josie greeted him as he and Buffy entered the house. "A letter has come for you by special messenger. He is waiting for your response. The letter is on the desk in the study."

"Very well. Thank you, Josie."

Charles was afraid of having his hopes built up, but one did not send a special messenger unless the message was urgent. He was at his wits' end in the search for Gardiner, and he could tell his sister was reaching her breaking point.

He recognised the scrawl on the letter immediately and ripped open the seal.

I've found him.
~Harris

"That is all I am to know? Has he spoken to him? Is he with him? Does he have his wits about him?" Charles slammed his fist on the desk. "What am I to do?" He stood, pulling the door open briskly, and walked out into the entrance hall.

"Josie? Where is this messenger?"

Josie came bustling out of the servants' quarters, wiping her hands on an apron. "He is in the kitchen, my lord. I thought to feed him while he waited."

Charles held out his hand to indicate he would follow her.

"Isaac Bishop, sir," the messenger said as he pushed his chair back from the table and stood up.

"I am Charles Winslow. Did Captain Harris say anything else to you? His message was rather succinct."

"Only that he expected you to come with me, and thought you might wish to leave your sister behind."

"How am I supposed to manage that? Where is the Captain?"

"Norfolk, sir. He is to sail as soon as you arrive."

Charles looked up at Josie in desperation.

She shrugged her shoulders. "All I know is, my Elly would want to go. I suspect your sister is much the same."

Charles inclined his head. "Would you please have our luggage packed?"

"Of course, my lord. Though I am sad to see you go, and I know my Sarah will be too."

"Thank you, Josie."

Charles walked back out to the front porch and began to follow the path toward the dock, the direction in which he had last seen his sister heading.

Sarah was again sitting on the swing, looking solemn.

"Has something occurred?" she asked. "You seem distraught."

"Indeed it has. We must be away to Norfolk immediately. Captain Harris has sent word for us to meet him there."

"Does this mean you are finished searching?"

He hesitated, for he was unsure what would be found. He did not wish to burden Sarah further.

"I do not know. There is a chance we will not return."

"I see," she said and turned away sadly.

"I must find my sister to inform her to prepare."

He continued down the path, wishing he had more time with Sarah. On their walks, she had been opening up more and had even shown hints of her old self. If he could convince her to join them…he balled up his fists in frustration. It was unlikely she would be ready to leave so soon.

He spotted Anjou some yards further on, walking slowly and looking dishevelled, with her bonnet in her hand and her hair loose from its pins. He could see she had been crying when he reached her.

"Anjou?" he asked with concern.

"I am ready to leave, Charles."

"What has happened? Are you certain?"

She nodded. "I am finished here. Can you make arrangements to sail?"

Charles could scream. Should he tell her? What if Harris only *thought* he had found him? What if he had not seen him? It would only break her heart all over again. He could see she had just put herself through hell making this decision.

"I have just had word from Captain Harris, in fact. We may join him in Norfolk."

"Where is Norfolk?"

Buffy says it is several hours south of here.

"Must we return with him?"

"No, you may wait here, but I must speak with him. It could be some time before we can arrange another passage."

She shook her head violently and he could tell she was struggling to fight back tears as her chin quivered and she turned her head away.

"I need to leave now."

He understood. He took her hand and walked her back to the house. *Please God, do not let this end in disaster*, he said silently to himself.

Chapter Nine

The carriage was loaded with their trunks, Charles had settled the accounts with the investigators, and they were saying their goodbyes. As they turned to climb into the carriage, they heard a voice call, "Please wait!"

"Sarah?" Anjou asked in shock. Did she realise they were leaving for good?

"May I go with you?" The look on her face was one of pure desperation.

Anjou turned to Charles, who was smiling at Sarah.

"Of course. I cannot promise this will be the most direct route to England, nor do I know what this adventure will hold."

Whatever did Charles mean?

"Charles! My courage may fail me. Will you see me back to England or not?"

"Yes, Sarah. It would be a pleasure to do so."

Anjou could empathise, though their stories were different. At this point, she only wanted to be home, and how would Captain Harris accommodate two ladies? Sarah appeared to need more help than she. Perhaps this would be a good reason for seeking another passage. She had heard Buffy speaking about Norfolk being a large port, so perhaps there would be more opportunities to seek a berth on a packet.

Sarah's trunks were strapped onto the carriage, and they were driven to the docks in Alexandria, where Mr Hutton directed them to another boat which was smaller than the *Wind*.

"We must *sail* to Norfolk?" Anjou asked. She was ready to board another ship if it meant she could be in England again, but she was less ready for an extra journey in the same manner. Having experienced an ocean crossing, the thought of being at sea in a small vessel was not pleasant.

"We will reach Norfolk faster if we do not have to stop for the night," Charles explained.

"Aye, miss. We will not go out into the deep. We will hug the coast and should be there by this time tomorrow. You could swim to the shore if you fell over."

She forced a smile. A joyous thought for one who did not know how.

They were soon ready to embark. In this boat, there was less room for all of them, and there were no bunks to be had; it was hammocks for each of them. In comparison, Harris's ship had been luxury.

There was much more motion in the boat, and so the party seldom spoke. Anjou had little idea how to help Sarah. She was battling her own grief and had not the energy to fight the other woman's, too.

Both sat quietly on the deck, since there was no room to sit in the cabin. As the sheets and rigging were being adjusted, they watched the men work, and held onto their bonnets as the wind caught in the sails. Anjou had witnessed none of this on the westward passage and she now understood why the men sang and chanted as they did. It was a Herculean effort to reef some of the sails against the wind. It also explained why a particular captain had looked like the god in the flesh.

Her brother had shed his coat and was lending a hand with setting sail, to Anjou's surprise. Sarah also watched with appreciation, and Anjou had to hide a smile when she caught the woman struggling not to look upon Charles. Anjou walked to the stern and surveyed the water as it divided into two streams behind them and they skirted the distant coast. She felt a small measure of peace, but not enough. Instead of the deep pain she had expected, it was as if she was enveloped in an obscure haze, walking around with an invisible wound she could not explain. She had thought she would feel differently. She stood alone until it grew dark. Charles had joined Sarah, where she sat on the deck. Sarah seemed to be more comfortable speaking with him, which should not be surprising— Anjou could always talk to him herself. Her brother was a good man, and this was the first time she could remember him looking at a lady in such a way. His eyes were filled with longing and admiration, and Anjou hoped he would not be hurt. She doubted Sarah would wish for another marriage now, if ever, after her first experience.

The thought made her wonder. Would she ever feel ready for love again herself? She had held her heart close for five years, though she had grieved and mourned. Of course, she had felt attraction, but it did not mean she wanted to go through this pain again.

A young sailor approached, to tell them a light meal was being served, if they would follow him. Anjou had little appetite for what she suspected the fare would likely be. They were shown into the small dining room of the Captain's salon, and were served a surprisingly luxurious dinner of beefsteak and oysters, with dishes of cauliflower and beans.

She ate what she could with her queasy stomach, and retired early to her hammock. She fell asleep and dreamt of Aidan again, but this time he did not recognise her. She awoke with a start, and realised it was only a dream; yet it had felt so real.

~*~

They arrived in Norfolk the next afternoon. The sails were furled, and they anchored some distance from land. The ladies had to climb down a rope ladder in their skirts, the sailors following behind with their trunks, into the small rowing boat. Once they had disembarked, Charles settled with the Captain, and found a cart to take them and their luggage to the *Wind*.

Charles went on board alone to speak with Harris, because he wanted to warn him there was not one, but two ladies in tow.

"Why the devil is *she* here?" Edward demanded. He must have seen Anjou in the cart.

"Anjou?"

"Yes, Anjou. Who else? Has she multiplied?" he asked with ill humour.

"Lady Easton's sister, Lady Abernathy, is also with us."

Harris cursed under his breath. "No. You had best book her on a packet straight to England."

"We came all the way here to find Gardiner, and you said you have found him. Why can you not take us to him?"

"I said I would take you, Charles. I left specific instructions for you to leave Anjou at River's Bend."

"How would I explain it to her?" He threw up his hands.

"What did you tell her, exactly?

"Nothing about Gardiner. She has finally given up and is ready to return home. I told her we had to leave from here. Sarah was in mourning at River's Bend. She is ready to return to England, and asked if she could accompany us. Now, what of Gardiner, so I may know what is best to do?"

"I found him on one of my runs in the West Indies in Bermuda. I tried to pay better attention, as I normally do not."

"Did you speak to him?"

"I did. I called out to him as old friends do." He hesitated.

"Out with it, man."

"He did not know me, Charles."

"Was it intentional?"

"If it was, he is the best actor I've ever seen. His eyes were blank, Charles. There was no recognition. I'd stake my ship on it."

"You have no doubt it was him?"

"None; the small birthmark beneath his left eye was intact."

"Deuce take it! What are we to do?"

"This is not my decision. I had thought to take you to see for yourself and decide what to tell your sister. I had not planned on a horde of ladies, however. The hold is full of cargo, as is every available space."

"I cannot leave them here alone!"

"I realise that," Edward snapped. "It is why I requested you leave Anjou at River's Bend where she would be safe."

"You did not elaborate. And you, of all people, should understand how stubborn my sister is!"

Harris sighed.

"Should I tell her?" Charles asked. "Or are we going to try to find him behind her back?"

"There is little chance of her running in to him, but if she ever found out we lied to her..."

"I have no intention of lying, but perhaps omitting. It is only that she seems to have finally accepted his death. What will this do to her?"

"I think you will have to let her decide for herself. She did come all this way, and he is her husband," Edward said.

"How did he come to be in Bermuda?"

"I did not have a chance to find out. I passed him on the street in Hamilton. My best guess is he ended up with one of the freed slave marine units who were given land in exchange for serving the Crown. Part of his face was scarred."

"He must have escaped or was found and rescued. We suspect Colonel Knott inflicted his wounds."

"The same Knott who shot Easton?"

"The very one." Edward remarked.

"Anjou and Easton's batman suspect it. He remembered some of that night. It places Gardiner there, at least."

"Either way, we still have a dilemma."

"I think we must take her to him, to see for herself," Charles said, resigned to the inevitable.

"The ladies will have to share a berth. I am taking a shipment to the island and it will be close quarters for a week until we arrive."

"I do not see any other choice." Charles frowned.

"Not unless you put Lady Abernathy on a packet," Edward suggested.

"I promised her I would see her home, and I feel I must see this matter through with my sister."

"It must be nice to be needed by the ladies," he said, his voice laced with sarcasm.

"It is astonishing how far kindness goes," Charles retorted.

"I am not unkind," Edward protested. "I may not be sweet, but I was brought up to be a gentleman."

"Which reminds me, Anjou was not at all pleased when she found out we had wagered on her."

"You were idiot enough to mention it? Neither one of us exchanged a pound," Edward protested.

"Her pride was wounded. And she was very angry."

"It was not meant to harm her."

"I know it and you know it, but she is very sensitive about her shyness."

"I will be a perfect gentleman. On my honour."

"I suspect it will take more. This will be difficult enough for her, so I beg of you, be gentle with her."

"How did I become involved in this again?" Edward asked as he looked heavenward.

Charles chuckled. "Because underneath the rough exterior is a diamond."

"I will do anything if you will stop your poetic drivel!"

"If I were a wagering man, I would bet you could not make my sister like you."

Edward grunted.

"It is perhaps not the time for wagers," Charles said with a sly grin.

"Let us find the ladies and be on our way."

Chapter Ten

On the docks, Anjou and Sarah were waiting in the cart with Hannah. It felt like Charles had been gone an eternity, but Anjou could see the *Wind*, and her brother's back. She was nervous, not only to be on the ocean again, but because she did not know how to behave around the Captain. It was unlikely she would be able to hide from him during a second voyage.

"What is taking so long?" Sarah asked. It appeared she, too, had been staring at Charles's back for some time.

"A good question," Anjou answered. "Perhaps they are rearranging the crew to accommodate us."

"Oh dear, I had not thought of being a nuisance. I sailed over with my father on a large packet ship."

"You are not a nuisance, but it is not a passenger ship. Captain Harris runs a merchant line, so you will not have a large, luxurious cabin as on some ships."

"I do not mind," Sarah said quietly. "I just want to return home."

"I understand." Anjou empathised. She could not get home fast enough either. She had been hoping her brother would book them passage on another ship.

Charles finally turned and looked over to them. Waving his arm, he made his way towards them, with Harris following.

Anjou's pulse began to race. She must face him.

"Ladies. You remember Captain Harris. Anjou?" her brother asked, failing to hide the mockery in his voice. She gave a slight curtsy to the

Captain, who was being introduced to Sarah. She watched him talk pleasantries with her, and wondered why she had not been offered the same courtesy before she embarked on her journey from England. Either Charles had bribed him beforehand, or Harris had decided his experience with her on that crossing had been pleasant... She almost smiled at the thought.

Charles took Sarah's arm to lead her to the ship. Anjou began to walk forward before she noticed the Captain had had put his arm out for her. She was so astonished, she stopped and stared at it.

"Am I to be denied the role of a gentleman?"

"I did not realise you aspire to it," she quipped before she knew what she was about. Her hand flew to her mouth.

He began to laugh. "A well-deserved hit. Now, please take my arm before my entire crew teases me mercilessly."

She took his arm and felt small and fragile by comparison.

"Are they vexed there shall be ladies on board again?"

"They do not yet know Lady Abernathy is to be a guest. I should warn you, it will be cramped until we set down in Bermuda to deliver some cargo."

"Bermuda?" She halted. "We can wait for a passenger ship. There is no need to trouble you."

"It is on the way to the Caribbean, where we can catch the westerlies and have a faster return trip than going directly east."

"That is good news, indeed."

"Bermuda is a beautiful island. The waters are crystal clear and brilliant shades of blue and green."

"Then I shall try to look forward to it. Shall I cook for you?"

"I picked up a new crew member who can cook until mine returns, though I shan't deny you if it is your pleasure."

"I am certain he will do better than I."

"He has yet to make a pie," he replied as he handed her to the gangplank to board the *Wind*, where Charles and Sarah waited for them.

"If you would not mind showing Lady Abernathy to her cabin, I must prepare to set sail. I would be pleased if you would all join me for dinner in my quarters."

"Thank you, that would be lovely," Sarah answered, while Anjou stood gazing as the Captain walked away, wondering what had come over him.

"Is something the matter, sister?" Charles asked from behind her.

"What has happened to the ogre?" she asked in return, turning to eye her brother suspiciously.

"I told you he could be nice," Charles remarked.

"Did you offer him a wager?"

"I will admit, I considered it. I decided it would be in poor taste in the circumstances."

"Indeed it would, dear brother—as would wagering on a sister at any time."

"Will you join him at his table? Or do you intend to stow away?"

"I suppose there is little harm if he means to be amiable, although I am much less inclined to socialise now."

"As I told Sarah, take one day at a time. The two of you have much in common."

"There are, perhaps, similarities. We have both lost a husband, but I cannot pretend to comprehend what her marriage was like. I scarcely had one, and I have no children."

"Whether or not you had different experiences, you both have to grieve and learn to continue with your lives."

She nodded. "Whether we want to or not."

~*~

The ladies were met with a different greeting from the one Anjou had experienced previously. She actually felt the crew seemed pleased to see her. Sarah received a few suspicious glances but there was none of the jeering or spitting of before. Anjou waved and smiled. She had never had much conversation with any of them, but knew each face. There was Biggs standing there with a smile, and Shaddock, who had once re-lit the stove in the galley for her, and who gave her a slight salute.

They made their way down the ladder to their cabin to refresh themselves for dinner.

"My goodness," Sarah remarked. "This is quite small."

"Yes, it is not what one is accustomed to. Hannah and I shared this on the westward voyage." She hated to think where Hannah might be forced to sleep.

"We might have to take turns while dressing," Sarah said, since there was scarcely enough space for both of them to stand up with the addition of their trunks.

"Yes, but I find there is little need to change often on board the ship. You will prefer simple, smaller skirts. I did not wear one gown from my trunk the entire trip," Anjou exclaimed.

Sarah looked surprised, but she nodded. "I have a simple dress or two. I have not been much in the habit of dressing for anyone but myself these past months."

Anjou nodded. "I will find Hannah and have her assist you."

"Thank you," Sarah replied as she opened her trunk.

Anjou went to find her maid. She found she was forced to go above board, for the normal passage through the tween deck was blocked with cargo. She climbed the ladder and found the men were still adjusting the sails. As she reached the main deck, she found herself standing directly in front of the Captain, who was at the helm.

"My lady?" The Captain greeted her with surprise.

"Yes, I was looking for Hannah's berth," she said, trying not to avert her eyes as she felt like doing under his penetrating stare.

"She is in the first mate's cabin."

"I beg your pardon?"

"Quarters are tight because of the cargo," he explained. "She will not be sleeping in the bunk with him," he continued with amusement, his eyes crinkling at the corners.

Anjou had to swallow her protest.

"She will sleep when he is on watch," he explained further. "It is not uncommon practice on a ship."

"Could you please tell me where she might be, then?"

"Behind you."

She turned to discover Hannah holding a rope while flirting with one of the mates. Anjou spun back to the Captain with a questioning expression.

"I do not believe Hannah will mind sharing her cabin," he said with a laugh.

"Sir!"

He shrugged his shoulders with a roguish grin on his face. Anjou was taken aback at the change in him when he smiled. His features softened and his eyes were twinkling with laughter, and she noticed a strange fluttering inside her chest. She quickly walked to Hannah's side. She sent her to help Sarah, then she realised she had nowhere to go until Sarah had completed her toilette. She found a place to sit near the hatch to the aft cabin, for there was nowhere toward the stern where she would not be in the way of the men trimming the sheets and adjusting the halyard.

She could feel the Captain watching her, and she struggled to remain aloof in her thoughts. She hoped her face was not pink with her discomfiture.

The Captain shouted orders, making her jump. "Starboard not larboard, Mr Gaffney! I do not wish to miss my dinner trying to right the ship!"

"Starboard, sir!" the mate repeated.

The terms were so similar, it was no wonder the man confused them, Anjou reflected.

She wished Sarah and Hannah would hurry. The boat listed to one side as the men twisted the bow and the wind caught the sail, and she held on to the nearest fixed object. Some of the men tied down the rope, while the others ran to the other side of the ship to begin unfurling a sail from another mast. It was so complicated, she was certain they would sink.

"Do not be nervous, they know what they are about," the Captain said to her. When had he approached?

"I wish I were not; it is worse when I watch them. I do not understand any of it."

"They are harnessing the wind so we may enhance our speed," he explained. "This ship can go against the wind, in a manner of speaking, if the sails are turned at the proper angles."

"I presume that is a good thing? And why this is reputed to be one of the fastest vessels?"

"Yes, indeed. It means less time spent on the water."

"I thought sailors enjoyed the water," she rejoined.

"It is an entirely different matter, sailing for business rather than pleasure."

"I had not thought of it in that way. I am terrified of deep water."

"It is good to respect Davy Jones's Locker, as we sailors refer to the deep. Can you swim?"

"No, it is not a pastime taught to ladies."

"For shame. It is delightful; you should try it whilst we dock in Bermuda. It feels like bath water there."

"I could not!" she protested.

"You could. My sister enjoys it at our home."

"You have a sister?" she asked in surprise.

He laughed. "Aye. Amelia. She will be out next year. I also have a younger brother, Simon, who is doing quite well for himself in the Royal Navy."

"Is it difficult to be much away from your family? I imagine they miss you."

"I do believe that was a compliment, my lady," he said. Suddenly, his eyes sparkled green.

"Take it as you must," she quipped, almost smiling.

"It can be a lonely occupation," he remarked as Sarah approached with Charles, indicating it was Anjou's turn to go down to the cabin. Sarah had dressed in a simple evening gown of lavender with a lace trim, and she looked beautiful.

Surprisingly, Anjou felt the conversation with the Captain was unfinished, but she was not one to display her curiosity by extending the exchange, and certainly not for a topic which was private.

"Winslow, would you be so good as to take over the helm while I change for dinner?" Harris asked.

"Aye, aye, sir!" Charles said with mock solemnity.

"You are to let Charles sail?" Anjou asked, feeling a surge of renewed terror.

"He is an excellent sailor," Harris explained.

"Edward taught me on the westward voyage, dear sister. Had you ventured above board for more than a few minutes daily, you would have witnessed it."

"This is not your first time?" she asked. She was unable to mask her disbelief.

"No, but fret not, the waters are calm. You may dress for dinner without fear of capsizing," he teased.

She gave him a scathing look and turned to go and change her dress. Captain Harris waited for her to descend the ladder first and held open her cabin door for her. Had there been a change in him, or had she been too proud before to give him the chance? Cat was there, curled up on her bed, and promptly jumped down to greet her.

"Ah, there is my old friend," Anjou said affectionately.

"The good-for-nothing rat-catcher has slept in your bed every night since you left," the Captain informed her.

"Cat has certainly grown fat," she said, scooping up the feline into her arms as Captain Harris left to seek his own cabin.

Hannah had put out a gown which Anjou had not worn since leaving England. She stared at the dress, her conscience warring with her. She felt guilt—she should be in mourning, as she had never been allowed to do so openly—when they had first heard the news, and there had always been the small shred of hope Aidan would be found alive.

For the first time since she had left England, instead of widow's weeds, she wanted to put on a beautiful dress. Seeing Sarah's transformation since they had first met made Anjou think about her own future. It was not as though dressing in a beautiful gown made the pain go away, but making the effort to care might be a small step towards healing.

She inclined her head at Hannah, who had been waiting for her approval. Hannah helped her from her serviceable and plain muslin dress into the pale blue silk with dainty sleeves.

"I am right happy to see you dress suitable for dinner. I hope this means your days of hiding and cooking are finished," Hannah said as she laced up the gown.

"Hannah, you are impertinent," Anjou reprimanded without severity.

"I know, my lady, but your *maman* is not here to say so," the girl replied as she took Anjou's hair down and brushed it to a silky shine.

Anjou knew her mother would have had much more to say than Hannah.

"I do not have anything to curl your hair proper, and I am tired of it being in a knot. Such pretty tresses should be shown to advantage, miss." Hannah began to dig through the trunk and produced a head-piece that was a simple vine woven with a few rose buds. She placed it on top of Anjou's hair, which still flowed around her shoulders.

"I think it's beautiful, miss," the maid said, surveying her handiwork.

"I cannot wear my hair down," Anjou protested.

"You cannot preach propriety to me here. You are only having dinner with your brother, Lady Abernathy and the Captain, who, as like as not, will still be in his shirtsleeves."

"Very true," she agreed. "Very well, I shall go as I am." She wished she had a looking-glass large enough where she might check her appearance. To be sure, she must look like a child beside Sarah, who was radiant and elegant tonight.

Charles and Sarah appeared as if they had dressed for a night out in Mayfair, which mildly annoyed Edward. He was not one for wearing his coat-tails to dinner while at sea. However, he did occasionally go to dinner or the theatre while in port, so he travelled with an evening dress-coat in his trunk. He had not shaved since they had left England and he called for Jones to help him change and trim his beard. He felt nervous, for which he ridiculed himself. It was infuriating he was attracted to Lady Anjou, who had scarcely noticed his presence, except to be terrified of him. Now Gardiner had been found, she would be consumed with him. Edward wished he could protect her from what was to come. Her brother should have heeded the warning to leave her behind. Had he known Winslow were to act thus, he would most likely have kept mum about finding Gardiner. It might not be honourable, but she would have been no worse off than before.

Anjou entered the salon and he could not take his eyes from her. He had always thought her uncommonly handsome, even wearing an apron and covered with flour dust. But tonight she looked like a mythical sea nymph emerged from the depths to tempt him. He adjusted his collar which was making it difficult to breathe.

Her eyes met his and they widened slightly, reflecting her own surprise at his changed appearance, which gave him some small measure of satisfaction.

They were seated at the table, and the steward began to serve them. As three succulent dishes of roast chicken, fillet of venison and buttered sole were placed before them, along with fresh bread and wine, he hoped Lady Anjou did not feel embarrassed for what she had prepared. They had just left port and so provisions were fresh for the first day or two.

Besides, anything was better than gruel.

"It appears the two of you are old acquaintances," Edward remarked as he noticed Charles and Sarah speaking with the easy familiarity of long friendship.

"Indeed we are, However, I had not seen Lord Winslow since he left for the war," Sarah said.

"A very boring topic, indeed," Charles added as he took a serving of artichokes from the dish and then served some to Sarah.

"I cannot imagine war would be boring," Sarah replied.

"He was not allowed on the front lines," Anjou remarked, "much to his disappointment."

"No thanks to my father's interference. I am the only soldier alive without so much as a scratch."

"Did you serve in the Navy, Captain Harris?" Sarah asked.

"I did, but set out on my own account after Napoleon's capture. My brother also serves and recently received command of his own ship."

"You must be very proud."

"I confess, I am," he replied with a half-smile. "He excelled quickly."

"Do you enjoy merchant shipping more than navy life?" Charles asked.

"I enjoy reaping the rewards of my labour more." He laughed. "And I enjoy escaping to warm climates."

"I noticed you take the more southerly routes across the Atlantic," Charles said.

"Wait until you see Bermuda. You will understand."

"Is it very beautiful?" Sarah asked.

"It is very likely the most beautiful place I have sailed to. I told Lady Anjou of its turquoise waters, and there are pink beaches and tall cedars.

But it is better to experience than to hear tell of."

"I am pleased to have the opportunity," Sarah said. "Will we stay there long?"

"We may stay a few days. There are some minor repairs and caulking I would not object to having carried out, so you may see the island. But only for a few days. I have goods to deliver."

"Do you exchange cargo in Bermuda?" Anjou asked.

"We do. I deliver cotton to them, which is large, and exchange it for spices and tea, which is smaller by comparison, so there will be more room when we return to England."

"I am not uncomfortable, sir," Sarah said kindly.

"Is everyone quite finished? Shall we play cards?" Edward offered.

"I think some after-dinner music would be pleasant. Would you and Anjou honour us with some pieces?"

"I do not play for audiences, Winslow," Edward replied defensively. "I am merely an amateur with too much time at sea."

"Please, sir," Sarah pleaded. "I have longed to hear music again these last months."

"I think it is a lovely idea," Lady Anjou surprised him by saying, while casting him a challenging glance. She had thrown down the gauntlet.

"Very well, if you insist."

"I do." Charles answered for her.

Edward helped Lady Anjou rise from the bench and she went to retrieve her viola. He took his violin from his cabin and arranged two chairs where they could be seated as they played.

"What is your pleasure, Madame? More Mozart?"

"Bach's *Chaconne*?" she asked with a hint of taunting in her voice.

"Of course, but I only know the arrangement as a solo piece. I do not wish to play alone."

"Then play it," she replied with a twinkle in her eye he could have sworn said, *trust me*.

As he began playing the opening notes of the profoundly moving piece, he wished he had never agreed to play with her. Hearing her before, through the ship's walls, had been stirring, but watching her interpret the piece and lend harmony to it evoked deep emotion within him. She played with raw passion, expressing herself in a way she had not with words. She forgot to be timid with the bow in hand, and she held him captive to the very last note. It was intimate, yet painful, to witness her emerge from her shell, only to know she would be lost to him in a few short days.

Chapter Eleven

Anjou was frustrated. She had experienced a connection with the Captain while playing, only to feel afterwards he was avoiding her. Had she offended him? Was she too transparent? She had poured her heart and soul, and much of her grief, into her music, and she thought he had felt it too. She always made a lot of her music, for it meant so much to her. Clearly, she was alone in her feelings. She was trying not to allow it to affect her, but while she was isolated on a ship with little companionship, there was little diversion for her thoughts.

When she returned to her cabin one evening, she found Cat lovingly licking two small kittens she had just given birth to.

"How tiny and precious they are!" Anjou exclaimed. One was pure grey like her mother, which she named Calliope, and the other was grey with stripes, which she named Triton.

"No wonder she wasn't catching the rats," Cook remarked when Anjou went to search for some food to take back to Cat.

"I imagine she will be back to work soon, and she will have two helpers before long," Anjou replied.

She was grateful for the diversion, for it seemed Charles and Sarah had become inseparable. Even when Charles took a turn at the helm, Sarah was there with him. Anjou did not avoid the deck as she had before, for the temperatures were pleasant and she enjoyed the fresh air. She spent some time in conversation with the pair, but she was beginning to feel as though she was the intrusive little sister. She read her books again and mended some sails and shirts for the men. Although they were all very handy with the needle themselves, it helped the time pass.

As they approached Bermuda, the waters began to change colours, and by the time the ship reached the shore the sea was indeed a turquoise hue. She had only once seen such a thing, off the southern coast of France. A warm breeze wafted overhead, and she was almost tempted to jump into the water. The shoreline was dotted with tall cedar trees, and stone houses painted in colourful shades. It was enchanting. What must it be like to live in such a small place, surrounded by the ocean?

The Captain was busy manoeuvring the boat to avoid the reef, and all the sailors were on deck to furl the sails as they closed in on the shore.

Anjou watched while a nobleman, dressed as he would be for a cool English day, greeted the Captain on the dock. There were many Negroes working there, and it seemed they were dressed more sensibly for the heat than he. Captain Harris and the man glanced across to where she and Sarah stood, still aboard the ship, and the man tipped his hat to them.

The crew began to unload the cargo into carts brought there for that purpose. Their personal trunks were also unloaded and after an open carriage arrived, drawn by two horses, they were finally escorted across the gangplank to the dock.

"Lady Abernathy, Lady Anjou Winslow, may I present Sir James Cockburn, the Governor of Bermuda."

"Ladies, it is a pleasure to welcome you to the islands," he said, bowing politely.

"Thank you, sir." Dropping into graceful curtsies, they responded together.

"My wife will be delighted to welcome some fellow ladies to our home. She longs for society from England."

"We will only be here for a day or two, Sir James. We must return to

England, but I promised the ladies they would see Bermuda," Captain Harris said.

"Then see it they shall. May I extend an invitation for tea tomorrow?" Sir James asked.

"Thank you, we would be delighted," Sarah said with rare animation.

"Please allow me to take the ladies in the carriage to the old Governor's mansion. The capital has now been moved to Hamilton, but we still entertain guests in St George's, and you will find all the comforts of home."

"Winslow and I will join you there later. We must attend to some business here first," Captain Harris replied.

"Excellent. You are familiar with the old mansion, I know. Until tomorrow," Sir James said, tipping his hat to the men.

As they rode along in the barouche, Sir James went on to explain about Bermuda's history and how it had become an English settlement by accident, when the *Sea Venture* had wrecked there on its way to Virginia in 1607. The islands had been a source of trees and food, enabling the English to survive while ships were rebuilt. This had eventually led to it becoming an English colony. Anjou listened while soaking in the warmth and beauty of the water surrounding the lush vegetation. When they crossed a wooden bridge, Sir James explained that Bermuda was actually made up of many islets, instead of being one big island as many people believed. Anjou thought it all fascinating, and that it could not be more different from England, until they pulled into the town of St George's where she could see the British influence, though it still had its own unique flavour.

~*~

Once the governor had driven the ladies away, Charles turned to

Edward. "Where do we begin?"

"It is a small place, and I am hoping a white man with a scarred face will not be too difficult to locate."

"You are certain he was not stopping here on business?"

"It is highly unlikely. Not many ships pass by, not since the war ended, and certainly not passenger ships."

Charles expelled a sigh. "I do not know whether to be grateful or not. Anjou seems to be healing at last."

"I have noticed," Edward concurred. "We must find him first, then it is her decision to make."

"Yes. Would the Governor be the best person to ask?"

"It is likely he would know, but he would also wish to know why. I do not want to stir up trouble for Aidan."

"Nor I. However, I want to know what happened. If my sister would be injured by his deceit, I would beg we depart and leave her in the dark."

Edward nodded. "I will begin by asking some of my partners in shipping. I will try to be discreet."

"May I come along?"

"If you allow me to do the talking."

"Of course," Charles agreed.

They began with the proprietor of salt, whom Edward knew better than the rest. They walked to his warehouse near the docks.

"Mr Joshua Moore, this is my old friend, Charles Winslow."

"How d'ye do?" The man greeted Charles cheerfully as he held out his hand. "What can I do for you, Cap'n Harris?"

"I met a man briefly when I stopped by last, but I cannot recall his name and I promised him some information."

"That does not sound like you, Cap'n."

"The heat here must be going to my head," Edward jested.

"Impossible! I never met a keener mind than yours. Well, what can you tell me about this man?"

"He has black eyes and black hair, very handsome, but the right side of his face is marred by a scar."

Mr Moore narrowed his eyes in thought. "You remember a lot about him to be forgetting his name."

"Incredible, is it not?" Charles remarked while keeping a straight face.

"He is a white man?"

"Aye."

"The only person I can think of is Henry Williams. He came some years back, with the Marines after the war. It was a sad business. He was injured in the war, and rescued and brought here. He did not know who he was or where he'd come from."

Edward and Charles exchanged glances.

"Where does he live now?"

"I don't know him well, mind you, but I believe he married one of the Tucker girls and helps run the plantation on the west end of the island, in the Port Royal area."

"I've heard of the Tuckers," Edward said.

"Aye, they own half of Bermuda."

"Married, you say?" Charles asked.

"If it be the man, yes. He keeps to himself, but he be right good with numbers and helps manage the plantation."

"Thank you for your help, Mr Moore," Edward said. He held out his hand to shake the other man's.

"Any time. I hope ye find him," he replied.

Charles and Edward left the warehouse and set off towards the ship, walking for some time in silence.

"This is bad news indeed," Charles finally said.

"We must see for ourselves first."

"And leave the ladies to their own devices?" Charles asked.

"It sounded as if the Governor has plenty of entertainment for them," Edward explained.

"It sounded to me as if he intends it for all of us."

"Perhaps, but I may plead work obligations."

"We must try. We are not here on a pleasure trip."

"I have arranged a business meeting, and you are considering investing," Edward proposed.

"I have no better suggestions," Charles remarked.

"It is best to remain vague. It is some distance from St George's to Port Royal. I suggest we make an early start."

"I am yours to command," Charles said, saluting smartly.

"Is that how Wellington liked it?" Edward teased.

"He could not care less," Charles laughed.

"You should have been a sailor."

"I might, yet."

"For pleasure, I hope?"

"Yes. I would not wish this lifestyle on a family, but I would enjoy sailing a yacht about on occasion. I am considering investing, remember?"

Edward shook his head. "If you are serious, I intend to add to my fleet. I have enough men I can trust."

"I will speak on it with my father when we return," Charles said thoughtfully.

"Are you considering settling down yourself?" Edward asked Charles in turn, as they climbed back onto the ship and prepared to move to anchor.

"I do not know if Sarah is ready. She may never be."

"She has been through much. Yet, she may not wish to return to England as Lady Abernathy," Edward observed.

"I had not thought of it in that manner. I do not wish to scare her away. She was not interested in me a decade ago."

"I would dare to say her eyes have been opened."

"I only wish I had been the one to open them," Charles said ruefully.

Chapter Twelve

Anjou dressed in a pale blue muslin for the tea she had little wish to attend. She had no desire to spend an afternoon with people she would never see again. It was too much effort. She would much rather wander over the islands and take in the beauty around her.

The carriage arrived to fetch her and Sarah as promised. She looked lovelier every day. Today, she wore a jonquil gown which made her appear youthful and her cheeks blossom. Anjou was happy Sarah had decided to proceed with her life. She only hoped her brother was not hurt in the process, for she could see he was smitten with Sarah.

The carriage drove them to Hamilton. A large house had been erected for the Governor and they were delivered to the front of the drive.

A pleasant Negro butler greeted them and showed them into an elaborate drawing room finished with ornate cedar accents.

Lady Cockburn and two other women were there as well.

"Lady Abernathy and Lady Anjou Winslow, my lady," the butler announced.

"Come in," she exclaimed. "We are delighted to have company. May I present Mrs Eliza Sanders and Mrs Mary Williams? They belong to our benevolent society. We do not have a large group, but we do our best. We are missing one member today, who is tending to a teething babe. Please, come take a seat. My Bessie lays a wonderful tea," she said as she stood and rang the bell.

"What brings you to Bermuda?" Mrs Sanders asked once they were seated.

"We are passengers on Captain Harris's ship, the *Wind,* and he needed to stop here on business."

"I am familiar with Captain Harris's trade," Lady Cockburn said. "We only wish he would stay longer."

"Yes, we have many young ladies who would be happy to make his acquaintance," Mrs Sanders remarked with a knowing smile.

"Were you visiting family in the Colonies? Two of my brothers now live in Virginia," Mrs Williams said.

"My family owns a plantation near Alexandria," Sarah explained. "I went there whilst in mourning for my husband."

"You have my condolences," Lady Cockburn offered sympathetically, as the butler brought in the tea tray.

"I accompanied my brother to search for a missing family member," Anjou said. "He was never found after the war."

"How horrid! I cannot imagine," Mrs Williams said. "My Henry was wounded in the war and left for dead. He was rescued and brought here."

"Mama, look!" cried a little boy as he ran into the room, followed closely by a governess.

"I'm sorry, ma'am, he got away from me," the bedraggled woman said.

"No matter, Sally."

"Daniel, you cannot run away from Miss Sally, and now you are interrupting our tea. Please apologise to the ladies."

"But I caught a frog, Mama," he protested.

"The frog is very nice, but it does not excuse poor manners."

He hung his head and said, "Yes, Mama." He turned to each of the ladies and apologised. When he looked up at Anjou, his black hair and black eyes reminded her so much of Aidan, she felt her chest tighten in pain and she struggled to maintain composure. Her chin began to quiver and her stomach churned.

"I-I beg your pardon, please excuse me!" she uttered as she hurried from the room before she embarrassed herself.

She had to overcome this, she told herself, as she escaped through the doors onto the terrace and gasped for breath. But why had a child, the image of her own oft dreamed-of son, appeared on this day of all days, and after she had resolved to let Aidan go?

She dabbed at the cold sweat on her brow with a handkerchief then walked along the veranda and out into the gardens, willing her heartbeat to slow, trying to master her emotions. She must, she chided herself; she must. Having taken several minutes, despite wishing to run back to the ship and sail away, she resolved to return to the drawing room. She walked back to the house.

"Please forgive me, I am still trying to accept my loss. It seems to come over me at the strangest times," she explained as she sat in her chair.

"There is no need to apologise," Lady Cockburn answered. Reaching over, she patted Anjou's hand kindly.

"I, too, am touched by the most unusual things," Sarah sympathised.

"Do you have other children?" Anjou asked Mrs Williams.

"We have a baby girl, but she favours me."

The ladies all began to discuss their children and Anjou tried to stay engaged in the conversation, but she agonised to herself, for the young boy's image continued to flash through her mind.

When the tea concluded, Sarah suggested they walk through the town and purchase some new hats of Bermuda plait which the ladies had enthused about.

Anjou purchased a fan and a bonnet, which she scarcely recalled trying on. She wanted nothing more than for the day to be finished.

~*~

"Good day," Edward said to the butler as he handed him his card. Charles did the same. "We are here to see Mr Henry Williams, if he is available."

"Yes, sir. I will enquire if he is at home. You may wait in here."

They were shown into an elegant parlour, which had a spectacular view of the harbour.

"Aidan appears to have prospered," Charles remarked.

"I would not mind such a place myself," Edward confessed. Then he noticed the portrait of Aidan with a lady and two small children.

The butler returned. "I am sorry, sirs. It would seem Mr Williams has gone to collect Mrs Williams and her children from tea at the Governor's mansion."

"Tea at the Governor's mansion?" Edward asked aloud, hoping he had heard wrong.

"Yes, sir," he said. "Every Wednesday she meets with the Benevolent Society there. I gather they were entertaining some English ladies today."

"Thank you for your help," Edward said, almost pulling Charles from the house.

A groom came running with the horses and as soon as he was mounted, Edward set his heels to the animal's sides without looking to see if Winslow followed. In seconds, he could hear Charles close behind. Neither said a word; they were galloping too fast for conversation and it was unnecessary. Edward knew they both realised the impending disaster, and did not wish Anjou to be alone for the discovery. Could fate be so cruel?

When Edward and Charles arrived at the mansion, they discovered the tea had finished some half-hour past. No one seemed upset or acted as if anything out of the ordinary had occurred, but they were informed the visiting ladies had gone to shop in the town for some of Bermuda's famous hats.

"Shall we look for them?" Edward asked.

"I believe so. I do think we must tell her or leave as soon as we may."

"I wish I knew what the circumstance was. It would ease my conscience. However, he clearly has a family now, and I cannot imagine your sister would try to separate them."

"No. I imagine my father can arrange an annulment since they were married by a Catholic priest."

"Can it be done quietly?"

"I hope so, given the marriage was secret to begin with. The Church of England would not recognise the marriage if it was challenged. I suspect it might have been intentional on my father's part."

"True, but how will your sister feel about it?"

"I cannot say. Perhaps we should set sail tomorrow and put Aidan behind us."

"If it is your wish, I will make arrangements," Edward suggested.

"It is," Charles replied.

"I believe I see the ladies coming from the milliner's."

Waving, Charles attracted Anjou and Sarah's attention. The two men walked towards them.

"Is your business completed?" Sarah asked.

"As much as it can be," Charles said vaguely.

"Would you mind helping me shop for gifts for the boys? I believe your sister is fagged."

"I would be happy to. Harris, would you mind seeing my sister back to the house?"

"Not at all. My lady?" Edward looked to Anjou.

She took his arm, but was clearly distracted. Charles and Sarah wandered away to visit the shops.

"Did you have a pleasant afternoon at tea?" he asked, all the while disgusted he was making small-talk.

"I managed," she replied and stopped walking. She clenched his arm tightly and he noticed her staring.

He followed her gaze across the street to where a lady and a small boy, who was the spitting image of Aidan, were walking hand in hand.

"Lady Anjou..." He began to attempt to distract her, but before he could finish, Aidan himself emerged from the shop. Edward would have recognised the face—the build, his walk—anywhere. He knew she did, too. He felt her knees weaken and he immediately held her up. "Do not let your courage fail you now," he whispered in her ear.

"What am I to do? He has a family," she said in disbelief. A tear fell from the corner of her eye.

Edward's heart ached as if he could feel her pain, and he wished he could have prevented this moment. He would give anything to take this from her.

Before they could react, Mrs Williams noticed them and began to wave.

"I cannot face him!" she insisted as they began to walk across the street.

"You must, Anjou, or you will never know. You will always wonder what happened."

"I cannot hurt his poor wife!" she objected and began to move away, but Edward held her firm. She was furious with him for not allowing her to flee.

"You came this far; you must see it through."

"I have! I see he has remarried!" She lashed out in frustration.

"Lady Anjou!" Mrs Williams exclaimed as she reached them.

"Be brave, dearest," he whispered.

"Mrs Williams," Anjou said, though he could hear her voice catch. "This is Captain Harris, whom we were speaking of earlier. This is Mrs Williams."

"A pleasure, ma'am," he said, tipping his hat.

"This is my Henry I told you of. You can see he was injured in the war. This is Lady Anjou Winslow."

Edward could see Anjou struggle to lift her eyes to Aidan's, though he did not take his eyes from Gardiner. Aidan's black eyes blinked twice at Anjou as if perhaps there was a hint of recognition, and then it was gone.

"How do you do, ma'am?" he asked with a slight bow as he took off his hat, revealing a large, jagged pink scar that was deep and ran from his eye to beyond his ear. Colonel Knott had not intended for this witness to live, if indeed he had been the culprit.

Edward felt Anjou's nails digging into his arm and he longed to carry her away, but she needed to know Aidan no longer existed.

~*~

Anjou wished she could die.

"When do you set sail to return to England?" Mrs Williams asked.

"By tomorrow," Captain Harris answered.

They tell me I am from England," Aidan said. "I do not recall anything before I lived here."

"How did you find yourself here?" the Captain asked.

"I was brought from the war in America," he remarked. "I was found injured in the river, in my uniform. It seems I floated face up until I was pulled from the water. They put me on one of the ships and brought me here."

"Yes, he was delivered to us after they arrived. My father was then the Governor. We knew very little about him. He was quite ill with brain fever for the first week. We did not think he would survive. When he began to recover, it was apparent he was a well-educated gentleman," Mrs Williams explained.

"The Tuckers had mercy on me and employed me."

"How fortunate," Anjou replied, hoping she was doing a good job of remaining impassive. Her insides were not, however. Her heart was racing, her stomach was churning and she felt as if she would be sick at any moment. He was Aidan, there was no doubt, though he had now filled out like a man, and was no longer the youth she had fallen in love with.

"Did no one report this to the British government? His family might wish to know he lives."

Aidan and his wife looked at each other. "It never occurred to us," she confessed. "I suppose we should consider it."

"Godspeed on your journey," Aidan said. "It was a pleasure to meet you both," he added, with the old familiar smile that made Anjou's heart squeeze painfully inside her chest. "Perhaps if you ever pass through again you will be able to visit for dinner," he added kindly.

"I will remember," the Captain answered.

Anjou smiled and turned to walk away, hoping Captain Harris would eventually follow. She could endure no more of this.

"Lady Anjou? May I have a word?" Mrs Williams called out.

No, she could not, she thought spitefully, but she paused and forced a smile. "Of course."

"May we walk a moment?" Mrs Williams led her a few paces away from where the men were speaking.

"I do not know how to ask this gently, so I will be frank. Is my husband the one you were looking for?"

Anjou was stunned. How should she answer? Her voice cracked when she replied, "Yes."

"What prevented you from saying so just now? Is there something he should not know?"

"I-I do not think it is best for me to answer."

"Is he your husband?"

Tears began to stream from Anjou's eyes. She had tried to walk away gracefully and leave this family in peace.

"Oh, no. Oh, no. What are we to do?" The woman began to grow frantic. "We have children! I am an adulterer! Or worse!"

Anjou wanted to slap the woman. How did she think *she* felt? She had waited five years for Aidan to return, only to find out now she had been living a lie.

"Mrs Williams, you must control yourself! This will not do! Your husband and children are just over there! You must now understand why I chose to remain silent."

She stood there sobbing and staring at Anjou.

"You are willing to walk away?"

"I see no other solution. He does not remember me—or our marriage. How could I separate him from the only thing he knows?"

The woman still looked astonished.

"I must go now," Anjou said. She was near to breaking, herself. She needed to be away from here.

"May I ask one more thing? May I know his real name?"

"Aidan. His name is Aidan Gardiner."

"Does his family know?"

"They do not know of our marriage. My parents thought to keep it private until he returned from the war. All I have is the marriage certificate. I will attempt to seek an annulment when I arrive in England. The secret is safe with me."

"Thank you," the woman mouthed to Anjou as her son began to call to her.

Anjou turned to walk with tears clouding her vision. She needed privacy. She needed to lose herself. She did not know how much more grief she could bear. In her mind, this had never been the result of Aidan's rescue. She did not know how to feel.

She began to walk as fast as her feet would carry her, not slowing until she made it to the pathway beyond the village. Finding a large rock beneath a tree, she sat down and gave in to the tearing grief.

Somehow, in the midst of her weeping, she was lifted on to a horse and managed to stay in the saddle long enough for the Captain to mount behind her. Feeling the warmth of his comforting arms only made her sobs worsen. He held her with one arm and the reins with the other. He managed to whisper soothing nothings into her ear until she was calm.

She saw nothing except Aidan's marred face as they rode, and she wanted no more of Bermuda.

"Take me to the *Wind*," she said at length.

"But..." He began to protest.

"Please," she pleaded. She did not want to beg.

He seemed to understand her unspoken reasons. She could not face others for the moment. He veered off the pathway towards the docks, where the ship was anchored. He slid from the horse with her cradled in his arms and carried her onto the ship.

Chapter Thirteen

Edward had watched the strength slip out of Lady Anjou as she had faced Aidan. All of her joy had gone. Then she had cried until she could no more, and had passed out from exhaustion as they had ridden to the harbour. He relished the feel of her in his arms while realising it was not how he would have wished the discovery of Aidan to come about. He reluctantly placed her on the bunk in his cabin, not knowing how she would react when she woke. She could be sullen or she could be angry—but he was afraid to leave her alone for fear she would hide in the tiny cabin again and wallow away in her grief.

He walked to his desk and dashed off a note to Charles. He would be wondering where his sister was by this time. Once completed, he went above and asked the first mate to see it was delivered, and also to make sure he knew they were to set sail first thing in the morning.

Returning to his quarters, he poured himself a drink and watched her sleep from across the cabin. Was there anything more painful than seeing the one you wanted wishing she were with someone else? Or viewing their suffering? If he was patient, would he ever find a place in her heart?

He observed the slight rise and fall of her chest with each breath. She had not moved since he had placed her on the bed, curled up like a small child. Some of her hair had fallen from its pins and her ebony locks surrounded her with reckless abandon. She looked so young and vulnerable, yet she had matured beyond belief since they had left England.

He could still see the redness around her eyes from crying—a stark contrast to her porcelain skin and delicate lips. He looked at her longingly in the fading light, knowing he was intruding, knowing she would be furious with him for seeing her thus.

How had he come to this? He had assumed her nothing but a spoiled miss when he had first seen her, just like the one he had been betrothed to when his father had lost the family fortune. But, despite his thoughts, he had stopped to speak to her. He had been drawn to her, even then.

He thought about everything that had happened with Aidan. He would never know for sure if he had made the right decision, but at least she would not always have doubts the rest of her life.

He stood up to refill his drink and lit the lantern. He might never have a chance to see her like this again.

He walked quietly over to her and pulled the coverlet about her. He brushed away the hair that had fallen onto her face, and she moved towards the warmth of his hand.

"If only we had met in different circumstances, my lady. I only hope there is enough room in your heart left for me." He longingly traced her lips and down the curve of her neck with his finger. He did not think it was possible for a woman to be more beautiful than she. In sleep, she resembled a porcelain angel, from the tip of her chin to the angle of her brow. He leaned forward and placed a tender kiss on the very brow which had a way of proclaiming what she often would not say with words.

"Rest well, my love."

Reluctantly, he walked to his bed, and removed his boots and waistcoat in order to settle more comfortably for the night. His eyes did not leave her until he could keep them open no longer and he was at last overcome with sleep.

~*~

Where was she? Anjou considered the question as she lay half asleep. Her eyes were heavy and reluctant to open. Feeling a rocking, she then heard a slight creak and realised she must be back on the ship. She inhaled and stretched... and detected a familiar scent. Cautiously opening her eyes, she blinked, waiting for them to adjust to the faint light. She was in the Captain's cabin! Squinting, she peered through her lashes, remaining as still as she could. That was when she saw him sitting up on another bed, asleep.

Anjou pulled the soft covering tighter and discovered she was still fully clothed. How had she come to be here?

It only took a moment for her to recall the events of the previous evening. Against her will, tears began to fall again and she could not help but sniff. As she wiped the moisture away, she looked over to see if he had heard. His eyes were open and upon her.

She bit her lower lip, but did not look away. His gaze was difficult to understand. Was it pity? She did not think him one to pity her. Yet he had been kind to her. He had taken care of her without a word.

Perhaps the look meant something more intimate, she mused, recalling the feeling she had experienced the night they had played Bach together. She was prodigiously confused, and suspected there was more depth to her feelings than there should be. How could she be so inconstant?

She broke the stare as another tear fell. He rose and walked to her, kneeling right before her and wiping the tear from her face. His gentleness was her undoing. In an instant he was cradling her as she wept—pulling the last pins from her hair and smoothing it, while whispering comforts in her ear.

"Let it all out, Anjou." And, "Hush, now."

131

"I don't want to. I hate to cry," she said, her cheek against his chest.

"But you must. It is necessary for you to heal."

"But he is not dead! I cannot reconcile how I should feel!"

"His body is alive, but Aidan is not. You know that, do you not? Aidan did not choose to abandon you."

"I know it in my mind, but my heart feels betrayed. For the past five years, my life has been a farce. I did not even deserve to mourn as a widow. It is now a mere disappointment I must overcome," she said bitterly.

"Your life is not a farce! You were true to Aidan, loyal. If any man should be so fortunate!" he replied passionately.

She was silenced by the quiet vehemence in his voice.

"Take your time. No one shall force you."

"No, but I need to let go of him. I have lost so much time."

"You need not let go of him. You cannot undo the past nor live in it," he declared. He pulled her away from the haven of his chest to look her in the eye. "And you can treasure your time with him instead of regretting it." His mossy-green eyes glimmered in the soft light of dawn, filled with compassion and....kindness. It could not be anything more. "I will leave you to compose yourself. Your brother and Lady Abernathy should be arriving before long, ready to set sail."

He paused to look at her one more time, then left the cabin. An unaccountable surge of anger swept over her as she watched him go, wondering what had just happened. Why was this man the one comforting her instead of her brother? She dried her eyes and resolved to stop indulging in self-pity; nonetheless, she was sad and felt sorry for herself. She had been loyal and true, and she could move forward with a clear conscience. It did not mean she could forget, but did she have to do so in order to be happy again? She thought about what the Captain had said about treasuring her time with Aidan. She thought she did, but being content with the conclusion of their story was her struggle. Her heart and mind battled one another, and only time would tell if one day they might accept it peacefully. She could not change the outcome, only live with it.

She stood and walked over to the washstand, where there was a small basin of water and a mirror. She gasped in horror at the picture she presented. How had the Captain been able to look at her so sincerely? She appeared as if she had galloped across miles of highlands with her hair unbound, to judge by the tangles now all over her head. And her eyes. They stared back at her with unfamiliarity—sad and hopeless. She looked a different person from the naive, idealistic girl she had been before the journey.

Anjou needed to do something. She did not know what, but something was building inside her which needed release. Her gown was impossibly wrinkled and her hair needed to be washed before she could hope to untangle it. How long would it be before Sarah, Charles and Hannah arrived? Feeling restless, she paced about the small cabin until she could bear it no more. She twirled her matted hair into a loose knot, thrust a few pins into it and almost ran from the small space.

She climbed the ladder to the main deck and was immediately struck by the beauty of the sunrise over the horizon. It stole her breath, being the most beautiful sight she had ever beheld. The sun was filling half the sky with a bright melon hue and its rays were mirrored in the water, which seemed to reach across the earth. She felt a sense of peace come over her, something reminding her that the sun would still rise and set regardless of her. It made her feel that maybe if she could survive this day, that every day hence would be a little easier than the previous one.

Captain Harris was standing alone at the railing, watching the same glorious vision. While she was not completely comfortable holding a conversation with him, he was not as daunting as he had been. He had shown her a different side to his personality and had supported her when her brother had not. She cautiously walked over to the railing some feet from him. She looked around to see no other men on deck. Had he not said they were preparing to sail?

"It is beautiful. I have never seen anything so majestic."

"It is one of the rare delights of the ocean."

They stood in companionable silence, and she wondered if she was interrupting him. He did not seem annoyed by her presence, so she spoke.

"Where is everyone?" she asked. Her voice sounded loud in the unusual quietness of the morning.

"I sent the watch away. The others are still sleeping off their last evening in port," he explained.

"Will it be long until the others arrive?"

"A few hours, I suspect."

She was desperate to leave this place behind her, and hopefully the pain that had been inflicted. But observing the calm waters relaxed her, and she even dared to lean over the rail to look down into the deep. The Captain moved closer and pointed out some fish to her that were swimming nearby.

She sighed. "They make it look so simple. It does look lovely to swim in—especially when I long for a bath."

"You will find no finer place to swim than here, I assure you."

"I believe you, but remember I have never learned the skill. I am terrified if I am not touching the ground."

"You should at least walk into the water from the shore. There is no one about to see this early."

"You are."

"I can be a gentleman. You may use the side of the ship to shield you, if you fear discovery."

She looked longingly at the crystal clear waters. It was tempting when the water was so still and she could see the bottom.

"If you are certain..." she said with hesitation.

"I am, but wait for a moment."

He went below deck and returned a few minutes later carrying some blankets and soap.

"I do not intend to bathe!" she exclaimed.

"Please yourself, my lady, but I intend to when you have finished."

What a strange way of life, she thought.

He helped her across the gangplank, and they made their way down to the shore.

He placed a blanket on the ground so she could sit down and remove her boots. As promised, he turned away and gave her privacy. She could not help but think back to when she had first fished with Aidan. She fiercely shook off the memory. Having removed her boots, she tied up her skirts.

"I am ready."

He turned and looking her up and down, tried to smother a smile.

"I beg your pardon! You are not supposed to stare! A gentleman would not have looked!"

"Forgive me," he said as he burst out laughing.

"You may turn around now," she said indignantly.

He did as she directed, but said, "What do you mean to do?"

"I mean to walk into the water to see how it feels."

"If that is all, then I will swim." He began to pull off his boots and she quickly turned her back. Did he mean to strip to his God-given suit in front of her? She heard him laughing, followed by splashing, and she stole a glance in time to see him fall back into the water. She longed to have the confidence to behave so recklessly.

She looked about and it was secluded; the beach was hidden by cliffs of boulders, and the ship was to their side, the windows looking out from the port.

When he appeared to be intent on swimming and paying her no heed, she walked to the edge of the water, which moved back and forth. Her toes sank into the sand as a small rush of warm water covered them. "Oh!" she exclaimed at the strange sensation.

Wanting to feel more, she glanced out to see where the Captain was. She could make out his head and his arms going in and out of the water. He was paying no attention to her, so she took a few steps until the water was just below her knees. It was a glorious feeling. If only she were a man, she thought, she could plunge into the water with abandon.

She had always ridiculed sea-bathers in England, who were devout in their devotion in the frigid waters there, but she could understand it here. She, who was afraid of water other than in a small bathtub, was considering it herself! If only Hannah were here, she might do it. She could touch and see the bottom, so it did not matter she knew not how to swim. She took two more steps, going deeper without thinking, even though it came over her skirts. She would gladly ruin this gown to feel this, just once. She was now up to her waist, and placed her hands on the water and turned around, laughing like a small child twirling in the breeze until an unsuspecting wave came over her and she lost her balance.

Two strong arms were there to catch her and right her, but she had taken in a mouthful of salt water. She coughed, trying to catch her breath.

He brought his palm briskly against her back until she calmed down. At once she became aware that her gown was soaked and he was bare chested. Easing back from him, she sank below the water.

"Are you all right?" he asked, concern etched upon his handsome face.

"I-I thought you were swimming."

"I was. When I saw that you began to go deeper, I came in. I never imagined you would go further than your knees while alone."

"I did not, either." She struggled to pry her eyes from his torso. He looked nothing like Aidan had as a youth. He had hair covering his large chest, and his arms were larger than her thighs!

He cleared his throat and she looked up at his amused face. "You might as well swim now."

How could he stand there, unclothed, without shame?

"But how?" she asked, completely distracted by his masculinity.

"With me." He took her arms before she could protest and began to lead her around.

"Kick your feet," he commanded.

She was too afraid not to obey, and kicked frantically, causing large splashes.

"Smaller kicks, please," he said as he squinted his eyes to avoid the errant drops. "Much better."

She relaxed as she realised he would not let go, his large hands encompassing hers. She even thought about the appearance she must present, but he did not look at her with disgust, only with tenderness.

"Next, you must learn to move your arms, but I think you have done enough for today. He eased her to her feet. "Stay here." He walked to the shore, and she watched brazenly as he emerged from the water, his well-muscled back and drenched buckskins clinging to his chiselled form. He was beautiful to behold, and she could not seem to remove her gaze from him. He retrieved the soap and returned to her. He did not take his eyes from her, nor she hers from him. Her heart began to pulse in an unfamiliar way and she wondered what would happen next. He reached for her and pulled the remaining pin or two from her hair, then started lathering the soap. Turning her away from him, he began to wash her hair. It felt more intimate a gesture then she had felt with Aidan in her one night as a wife, yet Edward was doing no more than acting as her maid. He leaned her head back into the water and ran his fingers through her locks, untangling the knots gently. It never felt like this when Hannah washed her hair. A mixture of guilt clashed with attraction—she knew she had put herself in a compromising situation. She closed her eyes when his hands stopped on her shoulders, uncertain of what to do next, or of what he would do. Did he think she was now a ruined woman and would be open to an improper relationship? The kindness of his actions did not seem as though he wished to take advantage of her, and he was friends with her brother. She felt his hands stop before she felt his breath on her neck. She remained still, unsure of what she wanted to happen as he placed a light kiss on her neck. Her insides fluttered as heat shot through her body, and she could feel her chest rising and falling rapidly. This man was affecting her in a way her husband never had and she was not sure how to reconcile her thoughts. Aidan was no longer hers. Was she disloyal for feeling this way?

"I will turn my back so you may get out. Cover yourself in a blanket and return to the cabin," he said quietly.

She nodded and did as he said, feeling bereft as she walked away from him.

Chapter Fourteen

Charles and Sarah walked down the main street of the town as Edward took Anjou away. He hoped Anjou would not be vexed with him later, though she seemed to have made peace with the Captain. There was no toyshop in Hamilton, but there was a haberdashery which had a shelf dedicated to items for children. There were tops and wooden soldiers, hobby horses and carved animals, more choices than he would have thought a young, small town would offer.

Sarah chose a skipping rope, a bilboquet, a Jacob's Ladder, and a new toy named a kaleidoscope, but still she appeared to be searching for more.

"It is not necessary to buy them every toy," Charles teased.

"I do not recall what my boys have," she said with a look of panic crossing her face.

"When I was about their age, my father gave me my first knife."

"A knife?" Sarah questioned. "They seem too young!"

"I imagine they have matured considerably in the past year, Sarah."

She looked away to compose her emotions.

"I am sorry, I did not mean to upset you," he said softly.

"Do not be. I need to recover from the doldrums and be their mother. Please pick out what you think they would like."

Charles selected a folding penknife for each boy, and a small gift for Anjou, and paid for everything. He suspected the shop owner had not sold this much in several months. He collected the packages, and as they left the shop, another family entered.

He could not control his surprise when he realised it was Aidan who held the door open for him.

"By Jove!" he exclaimed, nearly dropping his purchases.

A young woman stepped towards Aidan in a protective manner, and looking down, Charles saw a small boy who looked just like Anjou's husband.

"Lady Abernathy, it is lovely to see you again. May I present my husband, Henry Williams?" the woman greeted Sarah.

She looked meaningfully at Charles and in that moment he realised she knew. He fervently hoped that his sister had made it to St George's without witnessing this.

"It is a pleasure to meet you, Mr Williams. We have been purchasing gifts for my sons," Sarah said.

"I am sure you are anxious to see them again," Mrs Williams replied. "Captain Harris said you are to sail tomorrow?"

"Ah, so soon. I knew we would not be here long," Charles answered, trying to recover as he endeavoured to remove his eyes from his childhood friend. Although he had known Aidan was alive, it did not lessen the shock of actually seeing him. It was, however, clear that Aidan had no memory of him. "It has been a pleasure to meet you, madam, sir," he said, trying to exit gracefully. He could see Mrs Williams was anxious he would give everything away. He smiled reassuringly at her and placed his hat on his head.

They took their leave, and he led Sarah as they went to hire a conveyance to return them to their lodgings in St George's.

"What happened?" Sarah asked once they were some distance from the shop.

Charles sighed. "That was Aidan, Anjou's husband."

"But he..."

"Yes. He is remarried. As you can see, he had no recollection of me."

"What a fix! Poor Anjou! Does she know?"

"I pray she did not run into them as we did. Edward knows, however, and is planning to sail as soon as we may. I confess, we spent the morning looking for Aidan. Edward had seen him on a run over here while we were in Virginia. He suspected Aidan had suffered an injury to the brain. He wanted to only bring me here to investigate, but I could not leave my sister behind. Or you."

"How horrible! Your poor sister!"

They climbed into a small chaise and begin to roll away from Hamilton. Sarah sat beside Charles, appearing thoughtful. He wished he could express himself to her. Watching his sister's heartache, and Sarah's, was a poignant reminder of how short life could be. He was approaching one-and-thirty with little to show for his life. Even in serving his time in the army he felt he had done little that mattered. Yet Sarah had given him no indication she felt anything more for him than friendship; her interactions with him were much like of his with his sister, he reflected. It was most depressing.

"Charles," Sarah said, interrupting his thoughts.

"Yes?" he asked, turning to look her in the eye.

"Do you intend to settle down soon?" She answered his question with one of her own, her eyes flicking back and forth, searching his face.

"I suppose it has come time for me to do so. I had thought I had found the very person, once upon a time."

"You did?" She raised her eyebrows in surprise.

"I did," he affirmed. "But she only had eyes for someone else."

"I see," she said, lowering her gaze. "Was it very painful, Charles?"

"Not as painful as watching what happened to her."

She swallowed hard; she seemed to comprehend what he was trying to tell her.

"You have been very kind to me, Charles. He was never kind. I do think I would still be sitting in the porch swing had you not helped me from myself."

"Sarah," he whispered gently.

"I am more remorseful than you will ever know that I was blind before."

"I do know. You do not owe me any explanations."

"I am afraid, Charles. I am afraid my sons will hate me. I am afraid I would be as wretched a wife to you as I was to Abernathy. But I am more afraid to return to England bearing that name."

"Do not ever think you deserved what he did to you because you were not a satisfactory wife, Sarah! The fault lay solely with him. Do you understand?"

"I want to, but I could never discover what I did to make him hate me so; what made him do the things he did." Her eyes were downcast as she fidgeted with the lace on her gloves.

"I am willing to take my chances, if you are able to trust that I will never hurt you."

"I am no longer the naïve child I was then, to be dazzled with looks and riches alone," she replied.

"Could you learn to love me, Sarah?" he asked bravely.

"I already do, Charles."

She smiled shyly at him—the first genuine smile he had seen her give since he had first loved her all those years before.

He leaned forward to gently brush his lips with hers. He was afraid of frightening her. He opened his eyes to see her reaction and a tear was falling down her cheek.

"Did I hurt you, Sarah?" he asked, his forehead still touching hers.

She shook her head, clearly trying not to cry. "No. That was the first time I have ever been kissed, Charles. I did not think I would ever have the chance to be happy again."

It was a good thing the blackguard was already dead. How could Abernathy have been so impersonal? Charles knew many men of the *ton* treated their wives thus and kept mistresses for their lascivious desires, but how could Abernathy not have seen the jewel he had in Sarah?

"Sarah, I will devote the rest of my life to making you happy. I do not think there is a greater gift you could give me than your love and trust."

She answered him by wrapping her arms around his neck and pulling him closer for another lesson in love.

~*~

Edward ran his fingers through his damp hair while he watched Anjou walk away.

"I will not be another regret for you, my dear. You must mend your heart, first."

He was the greatest fool ever to live. Why had he put himself through the temptation? Besides her hair having been tangled into an adorable mess, he was desperate enough to take what little she could give him. He knew he could have taken advantage of her fragile state just now, but he had enough self-respect to refrain. Just enough. He had lived sufficient time in the world to know when someone desired him, but desire alone was not what he sought. And it would be wrong. Her sapphire eyes had looked at him with such trust and innocence...

He ducked himself beneath the surface, and stayed in the water to swim off some of his frustration, wishing he had the wisdom and strength of will to deal with the situation properly. They were due another three weeks of close proximity, and she seemed to have overcome her fear of him. Charles would be no chaperone at all with his undisguised admiration for Lady Abernathy. He would have to live with himself long after the journey had ended, and Lady Anjou had left.

The thought of her leaving him felt like a punch to the gut, worse than any sabre wounds inflicted upon him by the French. He slammed his fist down on the water as he emerged to return to the ship. He would have plenty of time to mull over his maudlin heart once they set sail. Charles and Lady Abernathy should be arriving soon, and he wanted to be prepared to depart as soon as possible.

"Harris!" He heard Charles exclaim shortly after he had changed from his wet clothes. He had half expected to find Lady Anjou in his cabin, but was not surprised she had retreated to hers. She had no clothes to change into, so he was thankful for the warm temperature.

"Come in, Winslow. I was beginning to think we would have to sail without you."

"I would not have minded, were it not for my sister," Charles said frankly. "I could stay here forever. The climate suits me well."

"It is one of my favourite places." Edward agreed. "Although there are some nice places in the Mediterranean."

"None so secluded. But it is not why Bermuda is my new favourite place."

Edward raised his eyebrows in enquiry but said not a word.

"Sarah has agreed to be my wife," Charles said, grinning from ear to ear.

"Congratulations, you rogue." Edward gave him a brotherly slap on the back. "I assumed it would be the case before too long. The two of you have had the stench of April and May since I saw you board."

"That's rich coming from you, my friend. It is time to find you a wife."

Edward's gaze shot up to his friend's. Should he tell Charles of his feelings? His intentions? Ha! No, he did not want what Charles would consider help. That was if Charles agreed with the match. Edward wrinkled his face. Would his friend consider him suitable for his sister? Were they in normal circumstances, would he seek permission to court Anjou? She was a widow. Or was she? Should he wait to go through the customary rituals when they were back in London? It seemed foolish after their experiences.

"Why the long face, Eddie?"

"I was considering what will become of your sister. Did you know we ran into Aidan as we were leaving town?"

"The devil! We did as well. I was hoping their paths did not cross. How is she? I should go to her! I would have come immediately, had you mentioned it last evening."

"She was not in the mood for company, Charles. You should realise that of your sister."

"Of course I do, but I am not company. I should be the one comforting her, not leaving her alone on a ship."

"I think I managed passably well."

Charles' eyes grew wide as he considered his friend. "Do you care to elaborate?"

"I let her cry on my shoulder. Nothing more.." Edward carefully omitted the details about her sleeping in his cabin and their morning swim together. He felt he had shown the restraint of a saint! He did not wish his friend to feel obligated to intercede on his sister's behalf. He knew Anjou would react badly to such an ultimatum. He did not wish to be hers by default. She had to want him—need him.

"Is she all right? I can see the concern on your face, Edward. Did something happen?"

"No, she was very brave. She walked away from Aidan and his new family with dignity."

"I should have listened to you and left her in Virginia," Charles lamented, pacing the cabin.

"There is no point in scrutinising your decisions now, Charles. What is done is done. Everything happens for a reason, and perhaps this is how it needed to be. Anjou always would have wondered, and maybe she would never have been able to proceed with her life."

"She has wasted her youth," Charles said sadly.

"It was not wasted. It has made her the woman she is now. I would rather her than a thousand schoolroom misses any day."

Charles looked up at him sharply. "By Jove, you are in love with her!"

Edward locked eyes with Charles. There was no point in denying his feelings. "I have come to care for her, yes. I am not ashamed to own as much. It does not mean I plan to take advantage of her vulnerability."

"I cannot wish for a life on the sea for her, Edward."

"Nor I," he said in earnest.

"I am astonishment itself! You would give it all up for her?"

"In a heartbeat. I can, and I will."

"Then you have my sincerest blessings." Charles held out his hand to him and they shook warmly.

"I should go to her now." Charles started towards the door.

"May I ask one thing?"

"Of course," he said as he turned back to his friend.

"I prefer to let her come to me in her own way. If it does not happen, I will withdraw graciously."

Charles swallowed hard, visibly moved. He nodded. "I pray she will see the prize right in front of her."

~*~

There was a soft knock on Anjou's cabin door. Hannah was just finishing combing the knots from her hair.

"Come in."

"There you are, Charles. You may leave us now, Hannah."

The maid bobbed a curtsy and closed the door quietly behind her.

"How are you? Edward told me you saw Aidan."

"Yes. I saw him and his family," Anjou replied calmly.

"Do you wish to speak about it?" he asked as he came further into the cabin and sat on the small bunk next to her.

"I do not think so. I think I will be all right. I have certainly spent enough tears. Captain Harris allowed me to cry on his shoulder without judgement and gave me some excellent advice. Would you believe he was the one to give me such comfort?"

"I tried to tell you he was not an ogre."

"I was very unfair to him. He has been kindness itself since we left Virginia. Perhaps I should apologise."

"You must do what you think is best. I am pleased to see you unruffled. I was uncertain how I would find you. I did bring you something from Hamilton."

He handed her a leather-bound journal.

"What is this?" she asked, fingering it gently.

"I thought it might help you to sort out your thoughts. I did not know at the time you had seen Aidan, but I do know putting my thoughts and feelings on paper has helped me through some difficult times in the past."

She looked at him with interest.

"Yes, your brother has feelings." He laughed. "Believe it or not, I have suffered disappointments."

"You keep them well to yourself, then. You always seem happy."

"I am happier now than I ever thought to be. Sarah has agreed to be my wife."

"I beg your pardon?"

"It is not a new fancy for me, Anjou. I have cared for Sarah for a very long time."

"Was she the disappointment?"

"Yes," he said quietly. "She was already betrothed to Abernathy at the time, and I was very young."

"She made quite an impression, if she is the one who drove you into the army."

"How did you know that?"

"*Maman*. And Aidan."

He sighed. "Yes. It was she."

"I hope she was worth waiting for. I am glad there will be a joyous end to this journey after all.

"Do not lose hope, sister mine," he said as he put an arm around her and placed a kiss on her head. "There is something in store for your happiness as well. I just know it."

Chapter Fifteen

Day One

Charles returned today with Sarah, and he brought me this lovely diary in which to record our return trip home. I have never been one to keep a journal as most ladies do, as I have always felt silly writing to myself. He tells me it will be helpful in sorting through my feelings. It is worth a try as I have little else to occupy my time.

My life is beginning again. I must insist upon it. I am not certain how it will be managed, but I must cease to think as I did of my life as being in abeyance until I found Aidan. I admit to myself I had been using him as a crutch, but that has been kicked out from under me. He is found, and he is a husband and father. He did not recognise me, and for this, at least, I am thankful. How much more injury would I have felt, had he deliberately chosen not to return to me!

Why does writing this on paper make it seem more valid? More absolute? Perhaps because I know I am returning to England, although not as Mrs Gardiner, widow. I will remain Anjou Winslow, now an aged spinster. I may find myself in Scotland alongside Margaux, as I do not think I can bear to go about in society as if it had never happened. I still have Aidan's picture and our wedding certificate, or I would begin to wonder if I had imagined the whole thing. I am holding on to the portrait in the hope that Captain Harris's words may one day be true.

Day Two

I confess, it is difficult to watch Charles and Sarah make love to each other every waking moment. They try to include me in whatever they are doing, but I am a dampener on their jovial mood. They cannot seem to help themselves, as it radiates from both of them. Sarah is a beautiful woman, and I can now see why Charles's heart was constant to her all of those years. I do wonder if losing Aidan has had the same effect on me. I am truly pleased for them, but it is not something an aching heart wishes to see.

Captain Harris has fashioned a perch for me on deck, so I may enjoy the fresh air and wind in my face. Thankfully it is some distance from the chickens, which have a very foul odour. Or is it fowl?

I have begun to learn the sailors' names. Connors is the first mate, though I do not see him often because he trades watch with the Captain. He always smiles and whistles a tune when he sees me, which makes the others laugh. It is not one of the tunes I am accustomed to. Perhaps I will ask him to teach me next time I am near him long enough.

Day Three

I now feel the boredom of long days on the water. I have spent most of my time sitting alone. I have had no interest in reading or sewing. My viola does not even tempt me to stir. Sarah's melancholy when we found her is much clearer to me now. I have adopted a similar refrain, as I have learned to stare numbly at nothing for hours. I feel as though I have naught to care about any more, although I know it to be false in my mind. The Captain says I must find a new purpose, and it is natural to feel this way after five years of waiting and searching for Aidan. Will I ever stop feeling this way? I do not know how to make it end. I must find an answer to the dilemma before *Maman* learns the whole, for she will no doubt have any number of ideas for pastimes with which to occupy my time.

Day Four

The Captain taught me to use a sextant today—at least he attempted to. It is much more complex to sail than I had considered, and it has to do with the sun's zenith at noon. The tool measures an angle, which tells you the position of the ship upon the earth!

He chatters on about longitude and latitude, chronometers and the genius of a Captain Cook, and even showed me how he logs the ship's position on the map each day.

I think he feels sorry for me and is making an admirable effort at preventing my doldrums...

We are now four days from Bermuda and he says we are moving at an excellent clip downwind. I take it to mean the wind is behind us, pushing us, rather than going against us.

Before leaving I had also feared other ships in the sea. During the war, there had been story upon story about privateers seizing vessels and sometimes their passengers. We have scarcely seen any other boats, except when in port.

Day Five

Tonight the winds have died down and it does not feel as though we are moving much in comparison to the past several days. The men were not able to have their music and dancing for a number of evenings after leaving Bermuda, since their attention was required to control the ship in the rough water. But last night I stayed on deck for the first time to join in, and even brought my viola to play along. Captain Harris played his violin more like a fiddle, while two of the men accompanied us with a harmonica and a flute. Hannah took turns dancing with some of the sailors, and Charles taught Sarah how to swing around on his arm in a jig-like dance she had seen the servants do at festivals and such. It looked like great fun as I tapped along to the rhythm. I actually entertained the thought of asking Biggs to join me for a dance, for I knew none of the others as well as him. I imagine he has two left feet, but at all events, I was saved from embarrassing myself by the Captain himself. It was most exhilarating to jump and swing around without a care for mis-stepping or maintaining perfect posture. I allowed myself not to care, and I enjoyed things as never before. The sailors were very pleased to see their master join in the dancing, though their extra ration of grog likely had much to do with their gaiety. And for the first time, I understood what a smile can do to me. Aidan's smile warmed me, but Captain Harris's set me on fire.

Day Six

It is difficult to sit idly by as I watch the men busy at their tasks, day after day. Every morning, they swab the decks and at a moment's notice drop everything to adjust the sails. The tasks look difficult as they pull and grunt with the exertions of their labours. I was laughed at when I offered to help.

I do wonder how I had thought the Captain a brute. I find myself watching him and staring. I cannot seem to control my gaze when he joins in to haul the lines or uses his voice of authority to shout commands. He no longer frightens me, since I have witnessed the tender side of him.

I had wondered, after the night we spent alone, if I would feel uncomfortable around him, for he saw my raw pain and grief. I have never allowed myself to be so vulnerable with another, save with my sisters. He has made no further mention of that night, nor indications of interest in me other than friendship. It is hard not to think of the morning in the water, when I was very aware of him as a man and he could very easily have taken advantage me. I am glad he did not, for I think I would have resented him for it. Now I am grateful, and cannot help but wonder if he would do the same for anyone he found in distress.

I have begun to dream again, but instead of Aidan's face, it is the Captain's I see. Is it true attraction, or is it akin to seeing an oasis in a desert?

Day Seven

The men can knit! It was raining today, so I stayed below deck. Hannah knocked on the door to ask if I had any threads that Raney, the deck-hand, could borrow. I had copious amounts of thread I had brought to ease my boredom, but had not yet touched. Nevertheless, a seaman knitting? This was something I had to see for myself. I was never more astonished in my life to see he could knit Belgian lace as fine as any found in the shops of Bruxelles. It seems all of the men can sew—they are usually the ones to mend the sails and their clothes.

Day Eight

The morning is heavy with fog, so it is another lonely time below decks. Charles and Sarah invited me to play cards in the salon, but I stayed in my cabin and read with Triton.

I have nothing else to write today. Captain Harris took the night watch due to strong winds and slept during the day. I had not appreciated how much of a comfort he had been to me until he was not there.

Later…

I spent the afternoon on the deck and I had a turn at the helm! I confess, I wonder what it would be like to be a captain's wife. Yet I cannot fathom being either separated for months or thousands of miles apart. Not again.

Day Nine

The clouds look differently today. They look like great fingers stretching out over the sky. It makes me feel smaller, more insignificant in this vast ocean than I already do. One of the sailors was warning it meant a big storm was *a-brewin'* but I pray he is wrong. My nerves may not be able to recover until we arrive in England. We have been most fortunate in the weather thus far.

Day Ten

The Captain married Charles and Sarah today. He says he does not have the authority to perform marriages, but he did it anyway. It was simple, but beautiful, as they recited the vows the Captain read to them. Charles said he and Sarah will be married properly when they reach England in order to satisfy the legalities of the peerage, but he did not want to wait to make Sarah his wife. Poor *Maman* will have to be content to hold a ball in their honour later. The Captain has graciously given his cabin to them and is sleeping in the mate's berth just on the other side of my little domain. They have asked to be set down in France so they may have some time alone together, and he may show her where we spent our childhood in Angers. I will be travelling alone with Hannah for the last day or two of the trip. I do not particularly mind as I have spent very little time with them since leaving Bermuda. The kittens are moving around; I think they will be walking any day now. Triton is my favourite, and Hannah adores Calliope.

The clouds are still strange in appearance today. I wonder if we may make it home before a storm.

Day Eleven

We said goodbye to Charles and Sarah at the port of Brest today. They seemed very happy and planned to return to England in time for her sons' holiday from school. Charles said he would write to our parents and ask Father to seek a house for them, and he promised to explain the whole of my dilemma so that Father may begin to seek the annulment from Aidan. Charles assured me it would not be long until we see them in England.

Charles also left me with a pocket pistol, in case of need. I cannot think what I could have to do with it.

By the look of the sky, I am tempted to stay in France until the storm passes, but the Captain wishes to press on. He attempted to reassure me by saying there was a storm on every trip, and if he waited for each one to pass, he would never complete a voyage.

As we approach England, I find the thought of returning less desirable than before. I have had much time to grieve and accept my new status, yet I do not feel ready to take my place in society again. I fear I will henceforth judge all others against the 'ogre', which has now become a term of endearment...

The winds have grown very strong, and the Captain has asked me to stay below, since the waves are reaching ten to twelve feet. He says he cannot be worrying one will sweep me away. It was the first time I have ever seen the slightest hint of anxiety on his face.

So here I sit, watching from his cabin, as the boat lurches and lists, worrying *he* will be swept overboard.

Chapter Sixteen

Edward's first thought when he noticed the brewing gale was to outrun it. After five years on the open seas, he was no stranger to a storm. But they were within two days' reach of England and he was growing desperate to have this voyage over with. *Why, oh why, must this happen with Anjou on board?* He valued her life more than his own, and he could not afford to think of anything but saving the ship and its crew and passengers. He had known the moment the skies had turned black and the air was filled with eerie calm that it was going to be a bad one. He knew Anjou had wanted to wait in port until it passed, but it was difficult to explain it could be worse to do so. He had a decision to make quickly: lay a-hull and wait it out or run off.

"Reef the sails!"

"Drop the anchor!"

"Heave to!"

His decision made, he shouted the orders. If Anjou had not been with him, he would have been tempted to run off, but he decided to go for the more conservative approach. They were too far from land to risk running aground on the rocks. It was going to be a very long night, and he would much rather be in the cabin with Anjou, holding her in his arms. It was too late for regrets, but he swore to himself if they survived the storm he would not wait another day to tell her–to show her–just what he felt for her.

Thunder began its ominous rumble in the distance and lightning began to streak its warnings across the sky. The winds immediately took their cue and started to howl and scream. The crew struggled to finish bringing in the sails and tie them off.

"Breakers ahead!" Gaffney shouted.

"Hard down, the helm!" Edward ordered in response.

The waves begin to form mountains and valleys around them. Everyone held on for dear life as the swell commenced its wicked dance of rolling the boat on its heel and back. There was little to do but wait, at this point, while controlling the damage and hoping the ship held together.

The rain began to fall in torrents, like sheets of needles shot into the skin. A large flash of lightning highlighted the deck only to show it awash with blankets of white foam.

He needed to check below to see if they were taking on water and the crew was able to keep up with the pumping.

Connors was manning the helm, so he shouted his intentions to him.

As he began to open the hatch, a wave lifted them up and promptly slammed them into a trough. He was unable to hold on with its bone-jarring force, and his head slammed into the side of the capstan. Holding his head, he swiftly closed the latch behind him and clutched on to the ladder as he regained his bearings. He made his way to the hull by jumping from post to post as the boat continued to be tossed about by the angry deep.

"Report, Anders!" he called from the passage into the hull. He could see that the situation was dire.

"We be taking on water, sir! We are at six feet and pumping as fast as we can, sir!"

"Keep up the hard work, men!"

The slamming of the hull must have cracked it open. The Great Deep was throwing her worst at them, and he feared the *Wind* could not withstand much more. He struggled to remain upright as another wave tossed them, slamming the hull down with a splintering crash.

His first thought was of Anjou, and he scrambled to his cabin.

"Anjou!" he cried, beating on the cabin door.

"Edward!" She replied frantically as she swung the door open. She grabbed a hold of him and threw her arms around him.

"Are you all right?"

She pulled him closer in response. He did not blame her when he looked around at the nightmare of broken glass and furniture.

"I do not think the ship will hold. You must dress warmly and prepare for the worst."

"What does that mean? I cannot swim!" she replied, her face etched with terror.

"I will prepare to let out the lifeboat. Put together a small bag with necessities quickly."

He pulled her to him and kissed her passionately, almost violently, with palpable fear in the air. He had to show her how he felt. It might be his only chance. She was shaking with fright, and one of the hardest things he had ever done was to leave her, but he was responsible for every life on the ship and could not stay with her as he wished. But he had just found her; he could not lose her now.

He climbed back onto the main deck as the ship keeled over thirty degrees starboard. This storm had been raging for what felt like hours already. If they could just hold fast a little while longer. He reached the helm, where Connors was struggling to maintain their position.

"How bad is it?" Connors shouted over the weather.

"We are taking on water too fast. We need to prepare to abandon ship."

"I never thought I would see the day. We must think of the ladies."

"They are preparing now. When the boat is ready I will go for them."

He shouted to the men to prepare to shove off.

"Aye, aye, sir!" They said as they scrambled to obey him.

Another violent wave lashed out at them, tossing them into the air. Edward could barely hold on with the force of the boat crashing back down on the water. He heard and felt the boat begin to splinter. They did not have much time left. He struggled back down into the ship to order everyone on deck. The men in the hull were still struggling but it was hopeless; the water was to their shoulders.

"Abandon ship!" He ordered down to them. Frantically, he hurried to his cabin to bring Hannah and Anjou up to the deck. They were both holding on for dear life, but were dressed in their heaviest garments and each had a small bag.

"Go above deck now and do not let go at any time! Do you understand me? If you let go you will go overboard!"

Hannah grabbed Cat and did as she was told, but Anjou remained.

"Go!"

"Not without you!"

"I am coming, I promise. I must gather some things from my cabin."

"Then do it!" she shouted. "I will not leave you!"

He did not have time to argue. He dug into his trunk for the bag he kept for this very situation. He found the pouch of gold and bills and tucked it inside his vest. It might be the only thing they could survive on if they lived through this.

He turned quickly, taking her hand as they made their way along the lower deck, and pulled her up the ladder. The water had already begun to take over the tween-deck.

As they reached the main, the wind was still fierce and the rain so hard it was difficult to see where to go. He grabbed on to the mast and pulled her close to him. He tried to look around to account for all of the crew.

"Is the lifeboat ready?"

"Aye, aye, sir!"

The decks began to bow as the pressure of the water threatened to open the ship to the sea.

"Where is Mallet?" he yelled as they began to load into the smaller boat.

"He and Smythe are in the rigging, sir."

He looked upward to see the men taking refuge in the ropes.

"Get your arses down from there! The ship is about to go!"

A loud crack rent the air and the mainmast came crashing down, tossing the two men into the sea.

"Men overboard!" As he heard the shouts, he felt his soul being crushed; hearing their screams and knowing he was helpless to save them.

Connors was attempting to steer to them around, which was impossible, and now the mast would serve to pull them under faster if the rigging were not cut.

"Get in the boat, Connors!" he ordered as he worked to slice the thick lines from the mast to buy them more time. He was struggling to keep tears of desperation and hopelessness at bay, needing to keep a straight head if any of them were to survive. Was there anything more desolate as to have a glimpse of hell opening its mouth to swallow you whole? He sawed feverishly at the lines until they were at last pulled away by the strong current. His worst fears had been realised; Mallet and Smythe had been pulled under.

The remaining crew and passengers were waiting in the boat, and he debated at what moment to give up and abandon the ship which had rescued him and his family from ruin. The sea continued to roar, as if taunting him. One look at Anjou and his heart decided for him.

~*~

In Edward's cabin, Anjou watched the hours tick by as she was tossed about causing her to be ill. She felt as though she had been at the wrong end of a fist in a prize-fight; her body was beaten and her equilibrium unhinged. Her worst nightmares had come to fruition—and those had not come close to doing justice to the reality of living through this. She felt completely helpless, for Hannah had been of no comfort once Edward had sent her to be with her. She could see very little from the windows, and it seemed as though darkness was covering them and water was seeping in. She had never before felt as though her life was about to end. It was more than sobering, and she did not know what to do. She could only pray and think on what she would do if she were allowed to live.

The Captain had come to her once, and had kissed her with such abandon she feared the worst. She could feel his anxiety as she, too, trembled, trying to savour the only taste of him she would possibly ever know. She had tried to stay calm and not panic as she had gathered her few necessities, although facing certain death was as hard to accept as the fact she was at Mother Nature's mercy. She could not even swim if she found herself in the water.

"If I must die, please let it be quick," she prayed, crossing herself.

Edward came back to collect her and Hannah, and she clung to him, knowing she was a burden but unable to let go. When he left her side, when one of the masts went down, she almost froze, yet somehow willed herself to be handed into the lifeboat. The minutes that went by as she waited for him to join her were the most painful. What would she do if they were separated? How were they supposed to survive on this small vessel when the larger one had been wrecked?

"Hurry, Edward," she whispered. She could feel the tension amongst those in the lifeboat while they also waited for him to board.

"What is taking him so long?" She finally asked the sailor near her.

"He is cutting away the lines from the mast so it don't pull 'er under faster."

Anjou did not understand.

"We need time to move away from the ship when it goes down."

At last he appeared and they began to be lowered into the water. As she looked down, she was overcome with fear and apprehension. The water was still choppy and angry. One small wave would take them under.

Edward lowered himself next to her.

"Whatever you do, do not let go. Water may come over you, but hold on to the bench or a rope. If we capsize, find something to float with. I will search for you," he instructed as he grabbed one of the oars and tried to push the boat away from the ship, which was beginning to split in half.

"Heave, men, heave!" He shouted as they struggled against the pressure.

She could only wonder what object might float as they rolled and bounced on the open sea. The waves were toying with them and she hung on with all her might. They watched while the *Wind* slowly began her descent into the deep.

Another wave lifted them up and set them back down roughly, leaving the small boat covered in freezing water. If the spray from the waves and rain had not been enough, now they were drenched.

Time and again this happened, and she could see the men were exhausted from the hours of fighting the storm.

The rain seemed to be lessening, though perhaps she was simply numb to feeling. She was cold and shivering, but still clung to the bench as hard as she could.

"Are you still with me, Anjou?" Edward asked her as he heaved an oar. "You must keep alert. Sleep will be the death of anyone who succumbs."

She struggled with heavy eyes, but tried to look at the others through the darkness. She could see that he was right. Those who had fought hard were growing weary.

She could not see Hannah, but hoped she was near Connors and he was helping her.

The last piece of the *Wind* slipped under and it seemed to take the worst of the storm with it. Everyone paused soberly to pay tribute to the loss. She could not begin to know how Edward must feel at this moment. She dared to look up at him, but his face was unreadable in the faint light. He finally stopped rowing and she felt the tension leave him. He relaxed and slid his arm around her and she sought refuge in his embrace. Her cloak had long since ceased to be of any use after the barrage of waves that had assailed them.

"Is it over?" she asked tentatively.

"I pray it is. None of us has the strength to fight another round."

"What will happen to us now?"

He sighed and took his time answering.

"It depends on where the storm left us. If we are not too far from shore we may be able to row in ourselves. If we are very fortunate another ship may see us and take us in. We will know more at daybreak. Stay close to me now, and I will tell you if anything happens." He kissed her gently on the head and exhausted beyond endurance, she huddled closer to him.

Chapter Seventeen

Edward fought to stay awake during the night, but knew it was too dangerous for anyone to sleep. The small lifeboat could hold more than these twelve people, but it did not mean it was comfortable, he thought, changing position to prevent his legs from falling numb. He held Anjou in his arms, attempting to keep his morose thoughts at bay. He heard a tiny meow and a hint of a smile teased his lips. He pulled back Anjou's cloak to find her kitten. Triton's eyes flashed at him in the darkness. How like her to have remembered this tiny life, too. He reached down and scratched the kitten behind the ears and felt him gently purring.

He was surprised to find only one cat with her, although when he considered the matter, she had not had time to retrieve the others.

The love she had for this small kitten made him think of the kind of mother she would be. He had never been a praying man, but he had to acknowledge they were fortunate to be alive, and he vowed to be a man worthy of this second chance, if they survived to see land again. Only about four-and-twenty hours prior, they had witnessed the union of Charles and Sarah, who were most likely safely oblivious to their plight. All he wished for now was a simple life at home with Anjou. He was mourning the loss of the *Wind*, to be sure, for it held many memories and had pulled his family out of debt. But he could buy more ships and continue the business, and would oversee it from England. The chances were he would never get Anjou on another vessel, and he would never leave without her again.

It was difficult to be alone with his thoughts. While he was grateful to have survived the storm, he could not help but think of the two good men lost. He had laboured and toiled to have a hard-working, trustworthy crew and he was equally hurt by their loss as he was his ship. He had seen gales before in the English Channel, but never one quite as fierce as this. He might have considered docking in France and waiting until it passed, had he known. It was easy to be wise following any disaster. He would make certain Mallet and Smythe's families were provided for.

He heard one of the men coughing, and it sounded like he had taken water into his lungs—a sharp reminder that they were not out of danger yet. Some could die of exposure or hunger if they were out here drifting for too long. The clouds had finally cleared, and dawn was breaking, allowing him to orient himself to north. He did not think they had travelled far enough to have left the Channel. They had been some one hundred miles due north of Brest—almost to England—when the storm had struck. With the anchors down they should not have been cast back out into the Atlantic, but it was disorientating and disheartening to endure a storm, only to be lost at sea and with little to sustain them.

However, they had been drifting forward, he thought, but it was difficult to determine without his sextant and map.

If they were in the Channel, normally he would expect to see other ships and boats passing. But, he was not surprised after a storm of that magnitude they had seen none thus far. He would like to begin rowing north if the men were able. If they were fortunate, they might run into a dory or brig before too long.

He looked down to find two blue eyes studying him. Anjou reached her hand up to the side of his face and he turned it to kiss her palm. There was little need for words between them; she seemed to understand he had been completely knocked-up and they were still in danger.

Having her near him was the only thing keeping him from sinking too.

She sat up and shuffled even closer to him, her head resting on his shoulder. She was still wet and cold. He opened his cloak to pull her in. They sat together, looking out over the sea in silence; he relished feeling her chest rise and fall in time with his. There was not a cloud in the sky and the waters were calm—one of the wonders of the sea he had yet to comprehend. Some of the others began to stir as the rising sun played gently upon their faces.

You been on watch all night, Cap'n?"

"I have."

"Ye shoulda asked me for a turn."

"I had much on my mind."

"I think we are still in the Channel, sir."

"I agree. I do not think we drifted too far off course."

"Then somethin' ought ta come by afore long!"

"We can only hope. We can try to row in and see if we are not closer than we think."

One by one the crew began to pull themselves together—Biggs, Cook, Connors, Hannah, Raney, Jones, Gaffney, Fetters, Tibbits, and Shaddock, the last coughing from having swallowed brine.

They must survive this. He needed Anjou to be his. In every way.

~*~

Anjou could not feel her toes and she was stiff and wet all over. She felt Triton move and meow, followed by a hand petting her. *I am still alive*, she thought as she opened her eyes to see Edward looking down upon her, raw emotion shaping his handsome features. He was exhausted and he looked vulnerable in a way she had neither witnessed nor envisaged before. Her heart lurched with love for this man.

She sat up gingerly and he opened his cloak for her to nestle into. It felt so strong and safe when he held her.

She looked out over the others, still huddled together in the small boat. Some had taken the floor and some had taken benches in their efforts to keep safe in the worst of circumstances. Hannah was also sharing a cloak—with Connors—and Anjou gave a sigh of relief. It would not have surprised her had some of the survivors slipped overboard from the small boat, given the waves that had washed over them. She was thankful it was not yet autumn or they would have surely died of cold during the night. It was so calm and peaceful this morning, it was difficult to believe these were the same waters that had roared and raged and swallowed the *Wind* whole. She offered prayers for their quick deliverance and decided to pray for Edward to still want her when this ordeal was over. She did not doubt he cared for her, but would he wish to spend the rest of his life with her? Those were questions she could not answer, and did not wish to ask him yet. He had much on his mind with the loss of his ship and some of his men. He felt responsible for the survivors' welfare, she knew, and would have to see to them before he could consider other concerns, such as she. She did not ever want to be away from him, but would he feel the same way? Would he want to continue seafaring?

As if sensing she needed reassurance, he pulled her closer. The men began to talk over their situation. Now Anjou moved away from Edward on the small bench; although propriety was a minor consideration at this time, she could not prevent herself acting from habit. She listened with half an ear, and longed to be in the comfort of his arms again.

Cook had begun to pass around some of the few provisions he had managed to throw in a sack. Anjou had yet to taste tack, and was thankful she had not before. It was a hard, flavourless biscuit and it was tough to chew. Some of the men dipped it in the water to soften it. She knew they could be some time on the water. As the men had been the ones to exert themselves, she declined most of her share.

When everyone had finished, Edward assembled the men to begin rowing. She stayed at one end of the boat, and Hannah was at the other, to be out of the way. The crew sang and chanted merrily as they worked, their mood infectious. They stopped and rotated from time to time, with a few minutes' rest in between.

Anjou kept her eyes forward, hoping to spy land and end the anticipation. Shaddock looked very ill but, despite coughing and wheezing painfully, insisted upon taking his turn at the oars. She was afraid the man was in desperate need of a doctor. She saw some seagulls, and once or twice thought she caught sight of land, but it was just a mirage, as she realised when nothing materialized.

How long could they continue like this? She glanced at the sun, which was not yet at its highest point

"Sail ho!" Edward shouted while she was looking at the sky.

It must be a fishing vessel, she thought, seeing tiny figures on a boat bringing in a net.

The feeling of relief that washed over her was indescribable. She had been beginning to fear they had lived through the storm, only to wither away whilst drifting on the open water.

Edward waved to attract the attention of the fisherman as the men rowed with renewed vigour towards the boat. He took command and negotiated with the master of the vessel, whose face was leathered and wrinkled. The man visibly relaxed when he heard Edward speak. He offered to tow them into Plymouth when he was offered compensation for his trouble. Plymouth was a few miles from their position off the coast of Cornwall.

They were pulled close to the fishing vessel and Anjou had to cover her nose. She had never smelled anything so noxious before. Her eyes were watering from the stench She and Hannah clung together, on the side away from the catch trying to contain the trio of cats. Hundreds of fish were in the net, some still alive and thrashing. The two of them watched as the small lifeboat was tethered to the fishing boat, and then they finally began to move towards land.

No one spoke much as they sailed up Plymouth Sound. Edward sat with the crew looking dejected. From the little that was said, Anjou surmised they were all surprised how close they had been to land, even though they had rowed some distance. It took no more than an hour for them to reach the shore. The ship pulled into the harbour and they quietly made their way onto the quay.

"The Black Bull is but a stone's throw away from the wharf. You'll find a friendly face and decent lodgings." The fishing vessel's master pointed a gnarled finger in a vague direction, shook Edward's hand.

"I am much obliged to you, sir," Anjou said, causing the old man to turn and flash her a toothless smile.

"Take care of yer lady, Cap'n," he said as he doffed his hat.

"Aye, aye, sir." Edward offered him a smart salute.

Carrying their meagre possessions, the crew began to make their way to the promised inn. They looked a sight, but Anjou hoped Edward's money would be convincing.

The innkeeper, a Mr Hill, eyed them cautiously but welcomed them when he heard their story. It was not a large establishment, but by then they would have been delighted with anything. The men were sent to the stable yard to swill themselves under the pump, and the weary travellers were shown to the few rooms the inn possessed to rest and dry their clothes while some warm food was prepared for them.

The inn was small yet cosy inside, with tables in the taproom and a private parlour to the side of the entrance hall. Anjou was led upstairs to a clean apartment containing a wide bed with blue twill curtains and covered in a plain patchwork quilt. A washstand and an oak cupboard completed the utilitarian space. At least it would be more comfortable than living on a lifeboat.

Hannah began to mutter and fuss to herself about what a shame it was to have lost all of Anjou's beautiful gowns. Anjou figured her maid was releasing her pent-up anxiety and let the girl continue. Anjou knew Hannah was as thankful to be alive as she was.

Releasing Triton from her cloak pocket, Anjou set him on the bed next to her where he was quickly joined by Cat and Calliope. All she wanted was to bathe and then see Edward again. She had no desires or worries beyond that. She would write to her parents, and ask him to post the letter for her. It did mean she had to decide what to do with her life before she saw them again.

The innkeeper's wife, a motherly, rotund woman, knocked on the door and brought in a tray with tea and fresh scones.

"I thought you might wish for some refreshment, my lady. The Captain was telling us all what you have been through, you poor dear!"

"Thank you, Mrs Hill. This is very welcome, indeed."

"I can have your dress laundered for you by morning. I can send something up for you to wear, if this is all you have."

"I have one other gown in my bag," she replied.

"It is in a sorry state, miss. It isn't fit for you to be seen in!" Hannah argued.

"The last thing I am worried about is wrinkles in my dress."

"You may press it while she bathes," Mrs Hill said to Hannah. "The Captain has ordered you a bath and the water should be up directly."

Anjou was touched he was thinking of her comfort even now when he must be beyond exhaustion. She had hoped he would be sleeping.

"If you see the Captain, please thank him for his kindness and tell him he should be resting. He kept watch all night."

The woman clucked dismissively. "He be down stairs arranging passages, writing letters, and calling for a doctor. But I will tell him you said so." She gave Anjou a smile and a wink, and withdrew as the servants entered with buckets of steaming water.

Hannah left to press her gown despite Anjou's insistence it would do as it was, so she slipped into the warm water and enjoyed it more than any other in her life—except, perhaps, her bath in the waters off Bermuda.

Having completed her bathing, Anjou dressed, then offered Hannah the use of the tub. She wished to venture downstairs to discover if Edward was still working. She could see her maid struggle between the need to chaperone her and her longing to bathe.

Anjou flashed her a big smile and closed the door behind her. Having washed and donned a fresh gown, she felt like a new person. She walked faster than was polite, but she was anxious to see Edward again. When she reached the parlour, however, it was empty. Her shoulders dropped with disappointment. There was still a small fire in the fireplace, so he had not been gone long. Maybe he had heeded her advice, after all.

"Are you looking for me?" His voice sounded behind her. She turned, to see him leaning against the doorpost, freshly shaven and looking more handsome than she could have imagined.

"Yes," she rasped.

He smiled at her, causing her insides to flutter.

"Close the door. Please."

"I do not think that is wise, Anjou. We are in England, now."

"Close the door," she said again, with conviction.

He obeyed, and the door shut with a soft click. She had his full attention and she could not form the thoughts she wished to say.

He was looking at her and smiling the smile she imagined Lucifer might wear as he tried to tempt a person into selling their soul.

She sighed loudly.

He stepped towards her slowly, only stopping when he was toe to toe with her. She looked up into those piercing eyes, their intensity scorching when they were focused solely on her. She reached up to touch his smooth face, studying every angle, every scar, wanting to know every inch.

"Anjou," he whispered as she licked her lips timidly in anticipation.

"Deuce take it, woman. You are making it impossible for me to remain a gentleman!" he growled. Taking her face in his hands, he kissed her hard, before settling into another slower, more sensuous kiss. Her hands wrapped around his neck and roved through his hair. She wanted him to understand what she could not seem to express with words.

He pulled his lips away but rested his forehead against hers and they watched each other for a moment.

"What happens next, Edward?"

"I must court you properly, my first attempt being an utter failure," he said dryly as he ran his fingers over her swollen lips.

"Consider me courted," she retorted.

"You forget your marriage to Aidan must first be annulled," he said quietly.

She pulled away and walking over to the fireplace, watched the embers smoulder.

Edward came up behind her and putting his hands on her shoulders, ran them soothingly up and down her arms.

"Now that I have found you, you will never be rid of me," he said. The deep rumble of his voice was reassuring, yet at the same time did strange things to her insides.

She spun about to face him. "What if they will not grant me an annulment? Will I be forced to love you from afar?"

"Never," he said, smiling down at her. Her heart leaped, but she ignored it.

"You need to sleep, and I need to find a Catholic bishop! How can you be so calm?"

"Because you said you love me," he whispered.

"How could you doubt it? I never kissed Aid—"

He placed a finger over her lips. "Shh. I know I said to treasure your time with him. That does not mean I wish for you to mention him during our intimate moments."

She could feel heat warming her cheeks and looked down. "Forgive me. I was only attempting to express my feelings for you—"

He hushed her with a soft kiss on her lips.

"I have written to Lord Ashbury, so if you would like to send your own note with my letter? I have explained our situation and planned directions. It is unlikely he will have received your brother's missive as of yet. I have asked for the message to be taken post-haste, and a carriage to be arranged for our travel to begin on the morrow."

There was a soft knock on the door. Anjou became conscious of her position and quickly moved to sit in one of the armchairs. Edward took a step away.

"Enter," he directed.

"The doctor is here, sir," Mr Hill said.

Chapter Eighteen

Edward left Anjou behind in the parlour to write the letter to her parents. He hoped the annulment would be granted quickly, or he would have to physically remove himself from her. She was not going to make being honourable an easy task. He had intended to give her time and court her properly in society, but surviving a shipwreck and seeing his life flash before his eyes had changed his best intentions. Still, he wanted to do everything properly.

Some time apart would be painful, but it would reassure him she truly wanted him. Her emotions had taken a beating, and she might have become enamoured with him because he was there, much though he loathed the thought. He prayed it was not the case.

He must visit his estate too, for if he intended to retire to it with a wife, he must ensure it was ready to receive her. His mother still resided there, though he thought she and Anjou would deal well together. His mother was not a strong woman, and he still partially blamed her for his father's undoing. She had taken a lover and started his father on his downward spiral of recklessness. Nonetheless, it was time to leave those feelings in the past, since he could not alter it.

He entered the small chamber where the doctor was attending Shaddock.

The doctor inclined his head in acknowledgement as he examined the patient whom Edward believed to be very ill. Shaddock appeared feverish and his eyes were sunken.

"It sounds as if he has taken in water to his lungs," the doctor remarked as he held his ear next to Shaddock's chest. Edward could hear the rattles from where he stood.

"We were shipwrecked, sir. Several waves came over our lifeboat, and surprised us. It is a wonder all of us are not suffering the same affliction."

The doctor nodded agreement.

"There is little more I can do, I fear. I am leaving a fever powder and expectorant. You may attempt to percuss the chest, but I fear the infection has already taken hold," he said quietly as Shaddock lay shaking on the bed.

Mrs Hill entered with a saline draught and barley water with which to tend the dying man. "You had best take yourself off now, Captain. I have strict orders to see you to bed. You will do no better here than I."

"Yes," the doctor concurred. "Mrs Hill knows what she is about. You do look exhausted, sir. You will be soon in his state if you do not take care of yourself. My orders."

Edward did not need to be reminded he was exhausted. He was afraid if he went to bed now he would not wake up for days.

"Perhaps a little rest would be welcome. I must see a letter posted, and then I promise I will be away to bed."

Anjou's note was waiting for him on the table in the parlour. He was disappointed she was gone, but he did not wish her to be alone here, either. He placed her note inside his letter and sealed it, and found the innkeeper to see it delivered as fast as may be to a destination over two hundred miles away.

He was beginning to grow weary. He had been physically exhausted before, but never had he been solely responsible with so little help. In the Navy, there had always been a complement of men to assist. He took full responsibility for each and every crew member, and also the full blame for their current situation. It was a heavy burden indeed. He must see that each was taken care of after they boarded the stage in the morning. He reached the apartment which he was sharing with two others. They had already given in to sleep. One was on a truckle, and one was on the floor, leaving the large bed for him. He barely had the energy to remove his boots before falling into a deep slumber.

~*~

Anjou decided to pour out everything into the missive to her parents. She had become more comfortable sharing her thoughts on the page because she had been keeping her journal. She decided it would be easier this way, than to have to recount it again once they arrived at her family's home. She knew her father was not one to make wise decisions quickly. The longer he could mull something over, the more rational the solution.

Dear Papa and Maman,

Before I say anything else, let me assure you I am in good health. I write to you from Plymouth, having survived a shipwreck in the Channel. Captain Harris has included in our plans a journey to London, thus I shall leave those details to him.

Charles is not with us, and he assured me he would write to you. I hope his letter has reached you, and I am not to be the bearer of his glad tidings. I will say no more.

Please do not be angry Charles left me. Hannah still attends me, and our separation was to be brief. No one could have anticipated such a tragedy on such a short voyage.

I will tell you the main of the story, for Charles assured me he would explain it all to you. We did find Aidan, but he had been wounded and suffered a brain fever that left him unable to recall his life before the injury. We found him in Bermuda at one of Captain Harris's ports of call, purely by chance. He is married and has a family. He had no recollection of me.

This was a difficult blow to accept, yet I believe so much time to reflect on the open seas has done much to mend my spirits. As you know, Papa, I must seek an annulment. I would hope this could be obtained quickly and quietly, considering the circumstances.

I do feel ready to continue with my life, which you will know when you see me.

With my deepest affection,
Anjou

She had not been as forthright as she had intended, but she had said enough. She was growing weary again, and decided she should leave the parlour before Edward returned. She did not want to keep him from resting. She folded the letter and placed it ready for him on the table.

The next morning, everyone assembled downstairs. Shaddock had not lasted through the night, and they had arranged for his burial at sea. The men had held their small ceremony for him early that morning at the docks, and it was therefore in a sombre mood that they said their goodbyes.

Anjou stood to the side, watching, surprised at her own feelings of attachment to each of the sailors. She had not known them well, but each had treated her with deference and respect.

One by one, they walked over to say farewell. By the time it was Biggs's turn, her eyes were struggling to hold back tears.

Connors was grinning when he stepped forward.

"It seems I was bad luck, after all," she said apologetically.

"That ain't nothing but a superstition, my lady. I'd say you were a great deal of luck," he added knowingly, inclining his head toward the Captain.

She blushed, but did not shy away. "I hope you prove correct, Connors."

Connors continued on to Hannah, who looked as if she would burst at any moment. Poor Hannah had fallen for him, with his dimpled grin and roguish manner. He led her away from the group with the obvious intention of speaking to her privately. Anjou hoped he could comfort her. Hannah would not be a pleasant companion if she was heartsick.

Anjou noticed Edward discreetly hand something to each of the men. She did not know what he was giving them, but she assumed it was enough to see them through the winter.

Her thoughts wondered to what would be next for him; would he truly give up life on the seas? She did not want to consider anything just yet. She only wanted to be with him.

The men boarded the stage, taking most of the remaining seats inside and on top, and Anjou waved to them as they rolled away. Edward had returned inside to settle up with Mr Hill.

Another hired carriage pulled forward for her to travel in with a sullen Hannah. She did not relish the thought of many days on the road, but she was ready to return to a more normal life.

A groom was leading a black gelding out from the stables, and she realised Edward meant to ride alongside. Her father and Charles seldom rode in carriages, either. She should not be surprised, but she was still disappointed. They were back in England and subject to all of the rules that went with it..

Mrs Hill had packed them a basket of goods to sustain them on today's journey. She and Hannah voiced their appreciation and climbed into the carriage. The postilion set the vehicle in motion and, while mindlessly stroking her kitten, Anjou watched for short glimpses of Edward through the window, and Hannah wept softly in the corner.

~*~

It took seven long days and nights before they reached Basingstoke. When they alighted wearily from the carriage for the night, they entered The White Hart Inn, grateful to be out of the conveyance and one day closer to London.

The innkeeper greeted them immediately by name.

"Lady Anjou? Captain Harris?"

"Yes," Edward answered with mild surprise.

"Please follow me to the parlour. There are guests awaiting you."

Anjou almost ran. She hoped it was who she thought it was. Her parents' faces brightened with obvious relief when she walked into the room. They stood up to greet them.

"*Oh, ma chéri!* I cannot believe Charles abandoned you!" her mother exclaimed as she embraced her daughter.

"I received your messages within hours of one another!" Lord Ashbury added.

"So you know the whole, then. We were almost home, so please do not blame him. He did ask me! I am hardly a green girl. And the sailors on board were perfect gentleman. Captain Harris runs a respectable ship."

Her mother eyed her suspiciously and carefully, as mothers were wont to do. "I do think you have changed, *ma fille*."

"I suppose I have, *Maman*."

"I am sorry about Aidan, *chéri*, " her mother said as she put a hand up to cradle Anjou's face tenderly.

At that moment, her mother spotted Edward, who had been lurking in the corner watching the family reunion.

"Lord Harris!"

Lord Harris? Anjou's eyes fixed on her mother. Had she erred? She looked to Edward, who did not seem flustered by the title.

"I have not seen you in a decade! Have you been hiding on this ship of yours?" Lady Ashbury asked as she went to greet him in much the way she would a familial acquaintance. She held out her hand to him and he took it warmly.

"I would not say *hiding*, but working," he corrected. "You have not aged a day, *madame*."

"I will admit, it gave me comfort to know Anjou was in your care once we realised Charles had left her," Lord Ashbury remarked.

"Where is Hannah, though?" Lady Ashbury asked.

"She has been with me the entire journey, *Maman*. She must be upstairs, laying out a change of clothes."

"Are you ready to dine? We can discuss more over some nourishment," her father suggested. "I had them hold back dinner until you arrived."

"Certainly. It has been a long week on the road. I had hoped you would be able to find us."

"If we may change quickly," Anjou said as they excused themselves to wash and dress for the meal. When they returned, Ashbury rang for a servant.

"We would have been with you sooner, but I was dealing with Anjou's predicament."

They paused the conversation while a hearty meal of roast duck, pheasant and chicken was served with an array of side dishes.

"Were you able to resolve anything?" Anjou asked anxiously.

"These things take time, dearest. But I was able to confirm Gardiner was Anglican, not Catholic."

"Why does it matter?" she asked with a frown.

"It means the marriage was invalid to begin with," Captain Harris answered.

She held her fork in the air and turned to look at her father. Had he known the whole time? Had she been living a lie for five years? She did not want to think too much about it. Nevertheless, she set her fork down carefully while assimilating it all.

"Do you mean to tell me I do not need an annulment? I was never married?" she asked with quiet disbelief when she wanted to shriek.

"I am not yet sure if it was a valid marriage. I am trying to make sure matters are handled properly and I have all of the information necessary to do so. A peer must be married in the Church of England, and as you know, your marriage to Aidan was arranged quickly, before his departure, with a Catholic priest. I have an appointment to speak to a bishop when we return, to see what must be done."

Her mother reached over and placed a hand on her arm. Anjou had lost her appetite. What must Edward be thinking? She was afraid to look at him.

"What are you plans now, Lord Harris?" Lady Ashbury asked.

He hesitated, and Anjou finally brought her eyes to meet his.

"I intend to take care of some overdue business," he replied vaguely.

"I imagine there is much waiting for you after a voyage," Ashbury said sympathetically.

"I hope it means you will visit your mother. I met her and your sister out shopping during the summer. She does miss you," Lady Ashbury said in a motherly tone.

"I had planned to, yes. It is long overdue."

Anjou's heart began to sink as he made no indication—or even a hint—at anything to do with her. She could not bear another loss so soon. She moved the food around on her plate.

"You will be surprised to know that your sisters have both married while you were away."

Anjou could not have been more astonished. She swallowed hard, but the lump in her throat was still there.

"I hope they have found happiness," she replied softly.

"You may see for yourself tomorrow, for they are visiting at Ashbury Place," her father said with a smile.

"Shall we remove, Anjou?" her mother asked.

All she could do was nod and follow her mother from the room.

The look Anjou gave him felt like a knife to his soul. Could she not understand why he was remaining silent? He wanted nothing more than to shout his love for her from the highest roof, but her marital affairs needed to be remedied, and she needed time to come to terms with all that had happened to her—even though it meant their being separated. He had to know she felt the same for him after some time to reflect. He would not hold her to a lifelong decision made under duress. And it had been duress—from when she had learned about Aidan, to their narrow escape from being shipwrecked in a fierce gale. He did also need to visit

Easterly Hall, and his mother.

A servant brought in a bottle of port and two glasses and took away what remained on the table.

Lord Ashbury leaned back in his chair after pouring each of them a glass. Edward wanted to speak to him about his own intentions toward Anjou, but it was difficult to know where to begin. He took a sip of his wine as he debated.

"Charles wrote to me, as you know..." Lord Ashbury spoke before Edward had arranged his thoughts. "Besides the unfortunate events with Gardiner and his unexpected marriage, he suggested you might wish to court my daughter."

Lord Ashbury believed in frank speaking. Edward could appreciate that. However, it was still a difficult subject to discuss with a prospective father-in-law.

"Yes. I do not deny it. However, I wish to do so properly, and after Anjou has had time to recover. It has not been an easy journey since we left England months ago."

Ashbury watched him carefully, and it was disconcerting. He outweighed this man by two stone and hovered over him in height, yet Edward felt small under his measuring gaze.

Lord Ashbury swirled his glass and finished his port before he spoke again.

"I think that is a wise decision. However, if I know my daughter, you had best not leave her to recover for too long."

Chapter Nineteen

Charles watched his beautiful wife sleep in his arms as the light of dawn crept into the room. His heart felt like bursting from his chest. He had not imagined his dream would ever become reality. He had thought his one chance for happiness had been lost to him forever. Oh, he was 'happy' and jovial by nature, but this deep level of love with someone who understood him, without conditions, brought inner contentment, and there was no longer a superficial mask to be shown to the world.

He had finally resolved he must settle on a suitable lady and wed for the succession's sake, and then he had seen Sarah again. All his old feelings for her had come rushing back. She had been far into the depths of melancholy, and he had not been sure if the Sarah he had known and loved still existed.

He still felt pangs of guilt for leaving Anjou behind, especially as an intense storm had rolled in not long after they had said goodbye in Brest. But they had not been far from England, or he would not have considered leaving her alone. But she had not actually been alone. She had been with Hannah and with Edward, who, any fool could see, was deeply in love with his sister. Even the sailors had teased their captain with a shanty about her when she was not around to hear it!

He and Sarah had travelled to the family estate in Angers. He had wanted to show her where he had spent his earliest childhood before leaving for Eton, and before his family had fled the terror of Napoleon. The estate had belonged to his mother's family, and they still visited from time to time and kept workers to tend to the vineyards.

It had been a blissful week of being absorbed in each other. They had spent countless hours together on the ship, and had felt restrained in the small space, while also being acutely aware of Anjou's pain. Here, they had the much-needed luxury of time spent wandering hand in hand through the open fields and vineyards, often without seeing another soul. Sarah continued to emerge from her cocoon as she realised he would not hurt her, but protect her.

"Good morning, wife," he said huskily as she began to stir. She was as fair as Diana in the flesh, lying here before him. He would never grow tired of seeing this first thing every morning.

She opened one eye and smiled ."Good morning," she said sleepily as she moved her body close to his. She seemed to be enjoying exploring marriage as a union of love and mutual respect as much as he did. She was utterly lovable and he still burned with anger at thoughts of how Abernathy had raised his hand to her and used her as a means to spawn his heirs...

"Why are you frowning?" she asked as she brushed away the creases on his forehead with her fingers.

"Forgive me. I let unwelcome thoughts intrude."

"We promised not to think of anything but the two of us for a few days."

"Guilty. I assure you, none of my thoughts of you are unwelcome."

"I do not wish for you to think at all at this moment, husband," she said, her tone husky and infinitely alluring.

"Your wish is mine to obey," he answered as he brushed her hair back from her face and looked at her tenderly. Would she ever know how much he loved her? He would tell her and show her over and over as long as he was able. He inhaled her fresh scent of lavender and soap deeply as he buried his face in her hair. She turned her face to his and his finger pushed away an errant hair, and then followed a path down her neck to her collarbone. Her eyes went dark with desire, and he felt a glimmer of hope she would be his wife in every way before long. She had made enormous strides since he had first seen her in the library at River's Bend, but he would not be the one to initiate their union. She must be the one to do it, no matter how long it took. It was a small kindness he could do for her when compared with all she had suffered. And it was vital to their future for her to know selfless, unconditional love. He would never take her out of anger, or use her as a vessel for producing heirs. Their children would be formed in love—or not at all.

"You are frowning again. Stop thinking," she commanded. Her hands slowly began to explore him, tentatively and softly. It was all he could do to lie there and allow it, for he wanted to reciprocate and his body was thrumming with desire.

"Charles," she said shyly as her voice shook.

"Yes, my love," his voice rasped.

"I want to love you back, but I do not know what to do," she said, with her cheek to his chest.

He took a deep breath. He had wanted this for so long. "Are you certain you are ready?"

She nodded against him, and reached up to touch his face. "Please, Charles."

His heart raced with nervousness as he lifted her and gently laid her on her back before him. He placed soft kisses near her ear and whispered, "I love you."

He proceeded to kiss her slowly and tenderly until neither of them could think of anything but each other.

~*~

Anjou slept fitfully that night, tossing and turning, trying not to dwell on what was to happen next. First, she tried a rational approach: Edward was simply visiting his mother and seeing to his estates. He would return to her shortly. Then an irrational fear ambushed her: *if he leaves, he will never come back*—one that was deep-seated because her experience with Aidan had left it imprinted on her soul. She must have finally fallen asleep some time near dawn, for when Hannah woke her, the sun was high and bright.

"Captain Harris is ready to leave, miss. You had best dress quickly if you wish to say your goodbyes."

Oh, the pain in her chest at hearing those words!

Had Hannah not been there to carry her through the motions, panic might have frozen her. The maid brushed and tied her hair into a loose knot and slipped a gown over her head before lacing its back. She slid her feet into her slippers without really registering and slowly placed one foot in front of the other as she walked down the stairs.

She would not fall at his feet and beg him to stay. What if their love was all one-sided and imagined in her head? She thought he desired her, but her mother had always said men were capable of separating desire from love. She stopped and squeezed her eyes tight and tried to shake the seeds of doubt away. She must remain strong and allow Edward to come to her in his own time. The thought of him not returning was unbearable.

If she had not known she would soon be in the bosom of her sisters, she would be in despair. She entered the parlour where breakfast was being served. Her mother and father were sitting with Edward, having what appeared to be a comfortable cose.

"Good morning, did you sleep well?" Edward stood and held a chair out for her.

She tried to quell the butterflies which were dancing inside her at the very sight of him.

"It took me some time to fall asleep. I apologise if I have kept you."

"Not at all. Shall I make you a plate?" he offered.

"I am not yet ready to break my fast. Do you leave immediately?"

"I should. It is two long days in the saddle to Chelmsford."

She wanted to ask him more about his home, his title, his family; she knew so little about his history, but now was not the time. She caught herself staring at him again, so she quickly averted her eyes.

"Would it be acceptable if Lady Anjou walked with me for a few minutes?" He looked to Lord and Lady Ashbury for their consent. How odd it was to be back in the stiff rigours of propriety after a taste of freedom!

"Of course. We shall prepare for our own departure while you do so," Lord Ashbury answered.

Edward held out his arm for her and Anjou placed her hand on it. They walked silently from the inn and down a gravel path to the privacy of a nearby park. The leaves had begun to turn, and there was a briskness to the morning air.

"I have been considering what to say to you all night," he began.

"And I have been wondering what those words would be," she admitted.

"It is necessary for me to leave you for a time."

"Is it?" She looked up and searched his eyes, which today were reflecting the grey of the skies instead of the greener hues of the sea.

"Anjou," he said as he looked tenderly into her eyes and ran a soft finger down her cheek, "do not make this harder than it is. After you have had a chance to recover—to consider—deuce take it, I am bungling this badly! Do you not see why I must go?"

She cast her eyes downward; she could not look at him. Her emotions were threatening to overwhelm her. She was trying to see his reasoning, to be understanding. She would not force him to stay if he needed time, but it seemed as if he was saying he was doing this for her.

He pulled her into his arms. "I knew this would be difficult." He sighed. "My feelings are constant, but I must allow you to know your own heart. You have been through too much too quickly."

"I have had nothing but time to consider!" she argued. She looked up at him pleadingly, no longer disguising the tears. She would let him see her anguish if it would help him understand. "My thoughts are only of you, Edward. How long before you will accept that I know my own heart?"

"Too long."

"Then why?"

"This is a small price to pay for clarity, though every day away from you will feel like a thousand years."

"I cannot change your mind, then? There is nothing I can say?"

He leaned down and kissed the tears streaming down her cheeks, smothering her face and neck with soft kisses before one last heart-wrenching embrace. She poured her very being into it. She wanted him to taste her long after he could not see her.

He pulled back, breathless from the intensity of their ardour. His hands cradled her face and he looked deep into her eyes. His gaze was imploring and tender.

"Please trust me, Anjou. We will have the rest of our lives together if you still feel this way when I return."

She could see his mind was set. There was nothing more to be said. They walked in silence back to the inn, where the groom was holding his horse. He mounted and tipped his hat to her, holding her gaze with one last, long, smouldering glance before riding away.

"Do not keep me waiting long," she whispered, watching him until he disappeared through the trees.

Chapter Twenty

It was with reluctance that Charles and Sarah began the journey back to England. It was necessary for her to face the demons that awaited her there, and to reunite with her sons. He trusted she would be able to face them more confidently with him by her side. He did not know her boys, nor what Abernathy might have done to them, but he hoped in time they would come to accept and even be fond of him.

They had written to her family as well as his, to inform them of their nuptials and intended return. Their plans were to head to Wyndham to visit her family and meet her sons before anyone else might have the chance to speak to them.

Now the day had arrived for meeting the children. Charles thought he was as nervous as his wife. Sarah had not remained still since she had risen that morning. They had arrived at Wyndham the previous day, and he could still not comprehend the welcome her family had given him. He had to admit, he had been concerned about their reception of him. He had worried they would think he had taken advantage of Sarah in her time of distress. He could not have been more wrong.

When they had greeted him and Sarah, there had been nothing but genuine pleasure and affection for her return and their marriage.

Andrew, Sarah's brother, had gone to fetch the boys from Eton for their short holiday. She had felt it best to not surprise them with news such as this in front of their peers. This would give them a chance to know Charles on their own territory.

Sarah kept walking over to the window every five minutes, watching the drive for any sign of their arrival. When at last the carriage pulled up to the house, Charles joined her at the window and watched as the boys alighted. She squeezed his hand so forcefully it hurt.

"They have grown so!" she exclaimed.

"Go to them, Sarah. You need your time with them first. You can tell them about us when the moment is right."

She nodded and gave him a quick kiss, before lifting her skirts and sprinting to her boys.

He continued to watch from the window as the joyous reunion took place. There was pure delight, and perhaps relief, on their faces, and Charles knew if he had done nothing else, bringing Sarah back to her children was enough. He expected it would not be easy for them to accept a new father, and he would tread cautiously, considering how he would feel in their position.

He would have hated anyone who dared to try and replace his mother. A grim reality.

He would have to make it clear he had no intention of doing so. Perhaps he would keep his distance and let them accept him in their own time. It was how it would be, anyway, would it not?

One could not force affection and feeling—it had to be earned.

He had been so lost in contemplation he had not noticed they had entered the house. The parlour door opened and Sarah was followed in by two rosy-cheeked boys.

"George, Lord Abernathy and Johnny, I would like you to meet Charles, Lord Winslow, my new husband."

So much for taking their time.

They stood silently assessing one another. Charles grew amused, as it reminded him of the British and French watching each other across the battlefield.

"I am very pleased to meet you, Lord Abernathy and Master Johnny." He held out his hand and each boy cautiously shook it.

At least they had manners.

"Why did you take our mother away?"

"Oh, George. He did not take me away, he brought me back."

George eyed him up and down, but did not comment further.

"Yes, well," Sarah muttered nervously, "we brought you some gifts back from our trip."

Johnny's face lit up while George's remained thoughtful.

"I am ashamed to say I do not know what you enjoy playing with these days." She sat next to Johnny, and was clearly trying to stop herself from smothering him. He did not seem to mind. Indeed, he appeared to relish his mother being near, in all likelihood soaking up her long-awaited affection.

Charles's heart gave a squeeze as he felt for what they must have endured.

Sarah stood and walked over to Charles, handing him the knives he had selected.

"Charles brought you something as well. I confess these were his idea. He said you were old enough, now."

Both boys looked up at him suspiciously. He walked over and placed a penknife in their hands.

He could see that George was trying to hide his pleasure. He smothered his smile as he went back in his mind to the time his father had given him his first knife.

"Thank you, Lord Winslow."

"It is my pleasure. Make sure you do not prove me wrong. It is a big responsibility to have a knife. You must use it wisely."

"Yes, sir," George said, fingering the animal carvings in the handle and playing with the clasp mechanism.

"Is there anything particular you wish to do during your holiday?" Sarah asked.

"Ride!" both boys answered in unison.

"You have come to the right place," Charles replied. "I imagine your aunt and uncle have special horses for both of you."

"Johnny gets to ride a horse. I am still on a pony," George said with his head down.

"It will not be long until you do, too," he said reassuringly.

The boy perked up. "Do you ride, sir?"

"Of course! But not so well as your mother."

"She is a bruising rider! At least that is what Aunt Elly says."

Charles laughed. "Then it must be so!"

"We may all ride together later, but I smell fresh scones. Is anybody hungry?" Sarah asked dismissing the compliment to her equestrian skills.

Both boys took off to greet the cook, who was just as happy to spoil them just as she had spoiled all the children of Wyndham.

"Everything will be all right, won't it, Charles?" Sarah asked wistfully as she watched her boys take off for the kitchen. They soon heard the patter of their feet running to join their cousins.

He took her hand, pulled her next to him and kissed her on the forehead. "Yes, I do believe it will."

~*~

Anjou's father joined her as she watched Edward go. He then led her to the carriage and helped her inside, where her mother was waiting for her, before closing the door and seeking his mount. Anjou was still reeling from what had just happened, but was determined to put on a brave face and remain optimistic.

"Do you wish to speak about it?" her mother asked.

"I do not think so. I believe it would be best to speak of other things."

"As you wish. Do you care to tell me about your journey at all?"

"Not yet. Tell me about my sisters. Who have they married? Are they men with whom I am familiar?"

"Indeed they are. You might be surprised, in fact."

"Then do not keep me is suspense! Margaux had forsworn nuptials, so do start with her."

"Do you recall meeting Dr Craig during our time in Scotland, at Lord Vernon's estate?"

"Of course! He was charming and kind," Anjou recollected with a smile.

"He inherited a barony upon the tragic death of his brother, and his estate borders our Breconrae."

"I am sorry for his tragedy. And the rest is history, I conjecture," she said with a sly smile.

"I must warn you, though, Margaux was badly injured in a fire. We almost lost her."

Anjou gasped. Had that been the pain she had felt in Washington and had mistaken for Aidan's?

"She has some scars, but they are becoming less noticeable now, and her maid is very skilled at covering them."

"*Pauvre sœur*." Anjou could not imagine. She resolved to stop feeling sorry for herself. Her troubles were nothing by comparison.

"Lord Craig was able to save her and they seem very well suited."

"I had always wondered why Lady Beatrice had given him up. Not that

I do not see Lord Vernon's virtues, mind you."

"Her heart was already spoken for," her mother explained simply.

"And Jolie? Pray tell!"

"This will be most surprising to you. Who could you imagine her with?"

"You would make me guess?" Anjou queried in disbelief.

"It is rather delicious," her mother teased wickedly.

Anjou listed off the few suitors she could remember.

"*Non, non, non.* Think of the unexpected."

"Do not tell me she is a duchess?"

Her mother smiled widely and nodded.

"*Mon Dieu!* Yardley?" Anjou asked, widening her eyes.

"The very one to tame her."

"I could not be more astonished!" She chuckled. "And you say everyone is at Ashbury Place?"

"*Oui.* Yardley and Jolie have just returned from a trip to France."

"I am very glad to know it. It will be good to see my sisters again."

She sat lost in thought for some time as she watched the countryside go by.

"Are they very much changed in marriage?"

Her mother considered the question some time before answering. "No more than you, *chéri.* But you will always be sisters, and nothing and no one will ever sever the bond you share."

"Yes, I expect you are right."

"I had despaired of any of you marrying, and now all of you have in one summer!"

"Not all, *Maman.*"

"I am confident of Lord Harris. He will not fail you. I quite admire what he is doing."

"Leaving? How is it admirable if it hurts so much?"

Lady Ashbury clicked her tongue lovingly. "No one said love was not sometimes painful, *chéri*. If you look to see, you will know this to be true."

"It certainly hurt to love Aidan, and my heart aches to be with Edward now."

"*Oui*," her mother whispered softly. "He must allow you time to know your heart. You must see from his view why this is important."

From his view. The thought echoed in her mind. Perhaps that was the missing key.

"Besides, *chéri*, he cannot court you openly if your marriage to Aidan has not been dissolved. Admire his restraint."

"Enough. I can accept we must wait to be wed properly. I cannot accept that I do not know my own heart. But I must respect his decision and try not to torment myself while I wait."

"*Ma fille*, try to sleep. You do not look well."

"*Merci, Maman*," she said dryly before giving way to the lull of the carriage.

~*~

Edward rode hard and fast for two straight days. He needed the reprieve from thinking that mastering a horse provided. When at last he reached his land, he stopped and dismounted to take it all in. He had not returned here since his father's death, when he had been faced with the grim reality of inheritance. Not only had he gained the privilege of a title, he had also held the debts. He had been left with no alternative but to seek employment or face destitution. He had closed up the main house and had been forced to let most of their staff go.

His mother and sister had removed to the Dower House, and he had purchased his brother a commission in the Royal Navy. He had then chosen his destiny with his own naval training and had sought out a new estate manager, who could look after his tenants plus attempt to make the three hundred acres prosperous again.

He had left for London, there to convince a bank to mortgage against the encumbered estate, which allowed him the purchase of a small ship. It was a miracle it had lasted until he had income enough to purchase *With the Wind*. He chuckled. He had set sail with a skeleton crew for the Azores, where he had begun trading exotic fruits to the wealthy houses of London. It had been a gamble, but it had worked. He had quickly expanded into salt and spices, and sometimes cotton.

He looked across his land from the woodlands, to the deer park, to the great house, and the fishing lake. It seemed a lifetime ago that he had been a part of it. He walked the horse as far as the lake to allow it to drink.

His mind went back to his childhood, when he had spent countless hours here, swimming with his siblings or fishing. He sighed deeply as an image flashed across his mind's eye of children with ebony hair and brilliant blue eyes laughing and playing around him.

He looked toward the house in the distance, with its yellow stone façade and columned portico that were still a testament to its former glory and grandeur. Everything appeared to be in good repair, at least, even if it was an empty shell inside.

He led the horse to the stable, where, thankfully, he found some hay for the animal and gave it a quick rub down. They did keep work-horses here for the fields, but there were no mounts in the stables now. He went on to the house, growing stiff from his ride. He entered through the back entrance, knowing he was not expected.

No one was about when he arrived in the kitchen, though there was a fire burning in the grate and he could smell some stew simmering. He needed to bathe and shave before calling on his mother. He would need to see to it himself. He wished it were warm enough to jump in the lake. He squeezed his eyes tightly as he thought of Anjou and how she had felt in his arms in the ocean. Was she thinking of him now?

He shook away the sadness and took two pails from the hooks on the wall. He filled them at the pump before hauling them back and putting them over the fire.

"Master Edward!"

He heard the shriek behind him and turned with a smile to see his housekeeper holding her hands over her chest.

"Bessie," he said affectionately at the sight of his old nurse, now housekeeper.

"You gave me a fright! Why did you not write to give me warning? The house is still in covers!"

"It is only I, Bessie. You know I need very little. I mainly came to check on my mother and see the state of the house."

She puffed out her chest a little. "You know the house is as neat as nine-pence. Why, it would be ready for the King tomorrow."

"I might hold you to that," he said impishly.

"You never would!"

"No, I never would," he agreed. "I am going to bathe and visit Mother."

"She isn't there anymore, Master Edward," the housekeeper said with a frown.

"Where has she gone?"

"She removed to London last spring, after Amelia left for school. Said she was lonely here. She didn't write to you?"

"She might have, Bessie. My mail goes to my London agent and I have yet to peruse it. I suppose I will see her later, then. Is Mr Chumley around?"

"Aye, but he's out with a tenant."

"Very well. If he returns, please tell him I would like a word with him."

Edward picked up towels and pulled the pails of water from the fire. The housekeeper clucked and attempted to take them from him.

"Ye shouldn't be doing for yourself, my lord."

"I do for myself on my ship, Bessie. Is there still a bath in my apartments?"

"Of course, my lord. I always keep your apartments ready for you."

"Very well. I shall return later for some of your stew." He gave her a wink and a kiss on the head before dashing off. He could hear her chuckles down the hall.

Edward took the long way to his apartments, despite lugging the heavy pails of water. His footsteps echoed through the emptiness. The furniture was shrouded in Holland covers, though the scent of beeswax and the gleam of shining floors attested to Bessie's care. He had never thought to come home again, yet here he was, with thoughts of bringing a wife.

He poured the steaming water into the tub, and went back to fetch more. When at last he stepped into the tub, it was a welcome reprieve for his saddle-weary bones.

He spent the next several days reviewing estate ledgers and visiting tenants—anything to keep busy and stop himself from riding back to Anjou. The estate looked well, and was thriving again, thanks to Mr

Chumley's diligent care over the years. Edward had poured every extra penny into reviving his lands, after the debts had been repaid, and it was now self-sufficient.

Every day he waited for news to come from Ashbury. Edward had told himself he must wait to reach out to her until she was free, and give her time to reflect in the bosom of her family. But would she feel abandoned? This was by far the hardest decision he'd had to make in his life thus far. The longer he was away, the more he wanted her.

One day, he was walking through the meadow, pondering his decision, when he spied some blue forget-me-nots. He smiled and reached down to pluck one. He could only think of her and the blue of her eyes flashing at him. It had to be a sign. He needed to visit London and his mother anyway...

Chapter Twenty-One

Darkness was beginning to fall when they drew through the gates of Ashbury Place, the family's country house not far outside London. Anjou's mother never liked to be far from Town. Anjou was fatigued, yet excited to see her siblings. They could hear their laughter coming from the drawing room as she and her mother entered the house. She hoped never to be separated from them for so long again, though she knew in her heart nothing could ever be as it was.

She walked into the drawing room and immediately saw the change in Margaux. It was difficult not to react, but seeing her husband dote on her eased Anjou's initial misgivings. Beaujolais looked every inch the Duchess, just as it should be. Anjou regarded Yardley and had to quell her instinct to be bashful, but if truth be told, Edward was more physically intimidating. Her sisters both came upon her at the same time and they locked together in a long embrace. She buried her face to hide her emotion. If only they could be alone again as before, even just for a short time. She had much to say and needed to be free as she could be with no one else about.

When she looked up again, she and her sisters were alone. Their husbands had quietly escaped to give them privacy. Perhaps there was hope, after all.

"We are so happy you are finally home!"

"I am relieved as well. *Maman* has told me you have both married. I was quite astonished, I assure you!"

"It is nothing compared with being shipwrecked!" Margaux replied.

"And after finding Aidan alive and married," Jolie added as she pulled them along to the sofa.

"This is going to take a while, I can see. Perhaps we should remove to your apartments, where we can be comfortable and have trays sent up," Margaux suggested.

"Will your husbands not mind?" Anjou asked.

"They will understand. We warned them how it would be."

Anjou sighed with relief. "I would like that very much," she said, and so they made their way upstairs to her room.

It was several hours later before Margaux and Jolie crept from her rooms to their own. She was much reassured about her sisters' marriages, having heard their stories. It sounded as though both could not be happier or have found mates who were more suitable.

Her sisters had expected her to be pining for Aidan, and had still not been told the situation of her marriage to him. She started at the beginning and told them everything, including finding Aidan and his new family in Bermuda. She had already confessed to them how her love for Captain Harris had grown, much to their astonishment. If only Edward had stayed with her, they could have seen for themselves and be reassured, just as she had been about them. She knew it was difficult for them to understand how her feelings could have developed for another person so quickly. It was not something she could explain, and was not something she had planned.

They did agree with his decision to give her time away from him. She wondered later if they would feel the same if they were in her shoes.

How long would Edward make her wait? Her father was to meet with the Bishop the day after next. She prayed there would be a quick resolution.

~*~

Edward arrived in London the next day and repaired at once to the rooms he kept there for convenience. His first call after that was to find Connors, to see if he would help him with a delivery to Ashbury Place. Something told him his mate would be more than willing to have a reason to visit a certain lady's maid.

That arranged, he set out to visit his mother. She had left a note with Mr Chatham, though it did little more than give her direction on Chapel Street. He dressed in grey trousers, a silver waistcoat and a black coat before tying his cravat. He decided to walk the few streets from his rooms in Bond Street to his mother's home near Buckingham House, hoping it would give him time to think of what to say.

The house was situated in a terrace in a new part of London. It was not unpleasing, though he would have gladly allowed her the use of the family residence once the tenants had vacated it. He wondered if Anjou would prefer living in town or the country. He had assumed the country, but it would behove him to ask before ousting his tenants.

He pulled up the knocker and let it drop. The door was opened by a butler unfamiliar to him. He placed his card on the salver held out before him.

"I shall see if her ladyship is at home," the man said with accents of arrogance. Should he bother to tell him he paid his wages? He was at least offered the kindness of being shown to a small study to wait, to one side of the entrance hall.

"Edward?" He heard his mother's voice from behind him. He turned to see a grey-haired woman who had aged much in the years since he had last seen her. She did not look like a woman who had deliberately ruined his family. She looked fragile and vulnerable.

"How are you, Mother? It has been a long time."

"Yes, too long, Edward. I am glad you found me."

"I went to Easterly, and Bessie said you had moved here. I have come to tell you I am taking a wife and returning home."

"Oh, Edward, that is wonderful news!" She made a move towards him and stopped herself. "I realise it has not been an easy task to recover from your father's debts. I am proud of you."

His heart went out to this woman. She had not been a horrible mother, and had likely looked for affection where she could find it. Heaven knew, his father would not have given it easily. It was time to forgive.

"I have not asked her yet, officially. But I expect her to accept." He felt nervous as he said the words, and hoped Anjou liked the gift he had sent.

"Would you care to join me for tea?" his mother asked.

"I would like that very much. You may tell me all about Simon and Amelia," he said, following her up to the parlour.

"And you can tell me about your betrothed. Oh, Edward, it is so good to have you home," she said wistfully.

"It is good to be home, Mother."

~*~

Anjou spent most of her days watching out of the window and it vexed her. Nothing had changed since Edward had left her, almost a week ago—except now she spent all of her time wondering when he would decide it had been long enough. By her calculations, it had been seven thousand years.

"This is ridiculous!" she exclaimed out loud. She had been hoping her sisters would be present for her wedding, but they were beginning to speak about returning to their homes for a spell before the Christmas holidays. Her father had met with a Catholic bishop, who had refused to annul the marriage without Aidan's presence, but he had suggested consulting an Anglican bishop, whom her father was meeting with today. She could not bear to think of what would happen if he also refused. Would they be required to send for Aidan?

No, she would have faith in her father's powers of persuasion. If Edward had been correct, her marriage would not be considered valid in the Anglican Church. Aidan would certainly not contest it.

At last she heard the distant sounds of a vehicle. She could not take her eyes from the drive as she watched while holding her breath. It looked like a hired hack from London and she wrinkled her face. She would not expect Edward to arrive in such a manner, and it was not her father. Perhaps Edward did not own a carriage? The conveyance pulled to a stop and a man—not Edward—alighted. He had a familiar look to him, but it was difficult to see the face beneath the hat. Anyway, it was not her captain or father, and so she gave up her watch and sat dejectedly in the nearby armchair where Triton was holding court on the head rest.

If she only knew where Edward was, she would be tempted to seek him out. No, no, no. This would never do. She must find something to keep herself from going mad. She would normally have sought out the comfort of her viola, but even that was lost to her. She rose, intending to find her sisters, who were likely in the company of their husbands, whom she needed to know better.

As she moved to the door, it swung open and Hannah stood before her.

"Oh, my lady! Look who is here!"

"Connors? What a pleasant surprise! Do come in," she said as she stood aside to welcome them into the room.

"How are you, my lady? This is a grand house," he said as he looked around, taking it all in.

"Thank you. Please take a seat." She indicated the sofa and sat down in the armchair across from them. "Would you care for refreshment? Tea? Biscuits?"

"No, thank you, miss. I have something for you. I hope I managed to keep them alive," he said self-consciously as he handed her a box.

"A gift?" She blinked in surprise and hastened to open it. Inside was a bouquet. "Forget-me-nots," she whispered. Her heart wanted to burst. She held them to her nose, which was not too pleasant, but they were not sent for their fragrance.

"The Captain brought them from Easterly, so he hoped you'd forgive them being a mite wilted," Connors said.

"I had not noticed. They are perfect. Thank you for coming all this way to bring them," she said with a smile.

"It was no trouble at all," he assured her.

"Hannah, would you like to have the afternoon off? I do not think I will have need of you for the rest of the day."

"Oh, thank you, miss!" Hannah smiled broadly.

"Please ask Mrs Winters to find a room for Mr Connors for the night. If you will excuse me now, I must put these in water," she said with a wry grin as she left, wondering where the man might fit in to her and Edward's future household as Triton jumped down from his perch and followed.

She placed her flowers in a vase in her room, and noticed through the window her sisters and husbands engaged in a game of pall-mall on the lawn. Oh dear. She hoped Margaux had mellowed a bit. She had always been fierce about competition. Anjou plucked one of the flowers from the vase and decided she might as well join the others.

"Anjou!" Margaux called out a greeting and waved when she saw her sister coming across the lawn. "I am just about to soundly rout Yardley."

Apparently, some things had not changed. Lord Craig looked at Anjou and winked. "You shoulda seen the row they had a few minutes ago, when he knocked her ball into the water," he said, his eyes crinkling in a smile.

"I did not break the rules!" Yardley insisted.

"My objection was to your ungentlemanly conduct!" Margaux retorted.

"Craig, if she were my wife I would take her over my knee…"

Jolie interrupted. "Now, now, it is only a game, my love."

Both Margaux and Yardley turned to look at her with astonishment.

"You may kindly refrain from comment, wife," he said sweetly.

Anjou and Lord Craig gave each other looks of bewilderment.

Margaux stepped forward to take her final shot. As she swung her mallet there was a well-timed cough, but the ball rolled perfectly through the final hoop.

"Nice try, Yardley. You had best learn some new tricks before next time," Margaux said, favouring the culprit with a dazzling smile. Anjou was happy to know she had not lost her spirit.

"Billards?" Yardley asked, without missing a beat. Clearly, he enjoyed the banter.

"After tea, perhaps. I need to rest for a while. Though I must warn you I am not too shabby at that pastime, either."

"Come, wife. Let us get you to bed for a rest," her husband said as he tucked her arm into his and led her away.

"Charming couple," Yardley mused as they walked away.

"There is nothing charming about watching either of you play together!" Jolie snapped back provocatively.

Suddenly, Anjou felt in the way and she was acutely conscious of missing Edward.

"We are going for a ride, if you care to join us?' Jolie asked her.

"I will stay here. I want to be near if Father returns."

Jolie reached out and squeezed her hand. "It would take your mind off your troubles."

"Likely it would, but I need my wits about me to keep up with you in the saddle," Anjou replied.

"Oh, very well, but I do not like to see you moping," Jolie said with a frown.

"I am not moping on purpose, dear sister. I pray it will be good news today."

"Forgive me. I know. I just want to see you happy."

"I am." Jolie cast her an unbelieving glance. "I will be," Anjou corrected. "I promise."

Chapter Twenty-Two

Edward paced and paced the floors in his rooms. Rain had begun to pour from the sky on his walk home from visiting his mother, and Connors had not yet returned from Merton. The blackguard was probably basking in the warmth of the Ashburys' hospitality at that very moment! He certainly would be if their places were exchanged. Connors had better be making headway with Anjou's maid, at the very least!

Edward stopped and rested his head against the window pane, watching the drops roll haphazardly down the glass as he debated the wisdom of his decision to wait. For years, he had not dared to dream as the bitter taste of reality had lingered long after his betrothed had abandoned him, when his father had died and left them in dire straits. He had never again hoped…and then Anjou had appeared out of nowhere to seek passage on his ship. Perhaps it was destiny, as she had declared that first day. He had finally begun to believe he would be with Anjou as her husband, but there was one more obstacle to overcome. He had been told an annulment could take months, even years. He knew he would lose his mind if he had to wait another week.

There was a soft knock at his door; it must be his dinner at last. He opened the door in his stocking feet and shirt-sleeves, to find Lord Ashbury standing before him.

"Forgive me for intruding uninvited," Lord Ashbury said.

"Not at all. I was only expecting dinner from the servant. Do come in," Edward said, opening the door wider. "Please take a seat. May I pour you a drink?"

"Brandy, please," Ashbury said as he sat in an armchair flanking the fire.

Edward handed him his glass and cleared away some papers before he sat in the leather chair opposite.

"I saw the Bishop today, and you will be pleased to know he granted the annulment. It required proving Gardiner was not Catholic, and explaining the delicate circumstances of his new situation, but in the end, the Bishop declared the first marriage invalid."

"I must admit I am relieved. I had heard these things can take some time."

"Donations to the church tend to help my concerns seem urgent," Ashbury reflected as he looked into his glass.

"I do not need her dowry, if it matters. I can even put a sum into a trust for her."

"You have managed to turn your father's losses around, then?" Ashbury asked, turning his gaze upwards.

"Yes, the estate is finally turning a profit and can continue without the income from shipping."

"Will you sell your concerns, then?" Ashbury asked, eyeing Edward closely.

"No, but I intend to oversee a fleet from England. I plan to retire from sailing."

"I must confess I am relieved to hear it. I would not wish such a life for my daughter."

"Nor I, sir. As I told Charles, it was a means to an end. I also told him he was more than welcome to invest," Edward added wryly.

"Now, about the wedding…"

~*~

215

A heavy rain had descended upon them the night before, and Anjou had decided her father was spending the night in London. She could not blame him, but she was tired of waiting to hear about everything that mattered to her. She ought to have the patience of a saint by now, but after enduring the shipwreck, she felt bolder and did not wish to wait for things to happen to her. In fact, she had decided she would go to London herself as soon as her father returned with news. She had some things she needed to attend to.

"Good morning, *Maman*," she said, entering her mother's dressing room, where her maid was styling her hair.

"*Bonjour, ma fille*," that lady replied lovingly.

"Have you any word from Father?"

"*Oui*. He stayed in Town and has more business today."

"Was there no word of the outcome of his meeting with the Bishop?"

"*Non*. His note was very brief."

"I am going to Town, then," Anjou announced resolutely.

Her mother turned to face her. "Why the urgency? Your father will inform your beau, and he will arrive. I have no doubts."

"There are some errands I must also see to."

Her mother looked at her through narrowed eyes. "*Très bien,* but you must not go alone."

"*Merci, Maman*." She kissed her mother on the cheek and went to order the carriage before making her way to the breakfast room, where her sisters and their husbands were conversing jovially.

Good mornings were exchanged and she filled her plate and sat down to eat with uncharacteristic haste.

"Anjou? Is something amiss? Or are you uncommonly hungry?" Jolie asked with a frown.

She shook her head and dabbed at her mouth with her napkin. "No. I am leaving for London shortly."

"London?" Margaux repeated.

"Yes. I have some shopping to do," she replied vaguely

"May I come with you? I also have some things to purchase before we return to Scotland."

"Of course. I would enjoy the company."

"Then I must go, too," Jolie added, clearly wishing not to be excluded.

"Everyone is welcome if you are ready to leave within the hour." Anjou rose from her chair and tossed her napkin on the table, before hurrying out to fetch her hat and pelisse.

A simple errand became the entire family removing to London. Her mother, once informed by Hannah that Captain Harris was now there, decided they should all return to Town.

The sisters left in one carriage, escorted by Yardley and Craig on horseback, leaving their mother and staff to follow shortly afterwards with the trunks.

Anjou had not anticipated the barrage of company and had thought she would have ample time to consider what she would say to Edward. However, the eight-mile journey passed quickly with her sisters' constant chatter.

"What is so important you must find it in London?" Jolie asked.

"My viola was lost at sea. I wish to obtain another."

"But it will take months for Amati to make you another!" Margaux exclaimed.

"Then I shall make do with what I can find for now. I do not wish to wait."

Margaux opened her mouth to object but shut it before speaking.

"Captain Harris plays the violin," Anjou mentioned casually.

"Does he?" Margaux asked with surprise.

"His violin also went down with the ship," Anjou replied.

They all sat silently, as if mourning the loss.

"Did not Papa speak with the Bishop yesterday?" Jolie asked.

"Yes, but he has sent no word," she replied with a hint of irritation.

"Ah, that is why we are going to Town, then."

"It might have played a part in my decision."

"Will your Captain return to you when it is resolved?"

"I do not intend to wait any longer," Anjou said with a sly smile.

"What are you going to do, Anj? A clandestine meeting is very unlike you!"

"I plan to seek out Papa first, but I shall send Edward a note to meet me in the park." She pulled the missive from her reticule and waved it around.

Margaux wrinkled her face. "I suppose we may be nearby so you will not actually be alone."

"I think it an excellent idea," Jolie exclaimed. "Though might we not send Yardley and Craig to be useful and invite him to do whatever men do? And we can accidentally meet up with them?" She winked for emphasis.

Anjou sighed. "I would wish for privacy."

Her sister's faces showed astonishment.

"Unfathomable, is it?" she remarked with amusement. "Though perhaps making your husbands useful is a good idea."

The carriage pulled up on New Bond Street in front of Leverne's music shop. Yardley and Craig had dismounted and handed their horses to the groom, to be taken to Ashbury Court.

Anjou went inside the shop, while Jolie and Margaux divulged their plans to find Harris to their husbands.

~*~

Edward had just completed the purchase of a sapphire ring for Anjou. All of his family's jewels had long since been sold off to cover debts, but he liked the thought of starting a new tradition with his bride anyway. He had been to three jewellers to find the exact shade of her eyes. He thought she would like it.

He exited Willerton & Green's with the small box tucked safely in his pocket. He had begun to walk south towards his rooms when he saw her—but with a handsome man he did not recognise. Should he confront her? No—yet he could not seem to keep his feet from moving forward. She turned, and he exhaled with relief. This must be one of Anjou's identical sisters. She had a slight scar on one side of her cheek and neck and there was no hint of recognition on her face, though she looked straight at him. As he walked closer he saw Yardley with another of her sisters on his arm. They were all so incredibly beautiful. But where was Anjou?

Yardley saw him and waved.

"Harris!" Yardley extended his hand. "May I have the pleasure of introducing my wife? This is Beaujolais. This is Lord Harris."

"Your Grace," he said with a bow.

"And my brother-in-law, Lord Craig, and his wife Margaux."

"My lord and my lady, it is a pleasure."

"Indeed it is. I believe you are acquainted with our sister?" Margaux asked.

"I claim to know both your brother and sister very well."

"Is your afternoon spoken for? We would be pleased to welcome you for tea."

"I had planned to seek out your sister at Ashbury Place, in fact."

"It seems that we have saved you a trip." Jolie inclined her head.

He turned to look as Anjou exited the shop behind him. His breath caught at the sight of her. To think she wanted him! He still could not quite believe she loved him—him! He, Edward Harris—the rough sea-faring brute, she had called him. A rare smile came to his face at the recollection. His heart was overflowing with a deep, unselfish love for this woman. He never wanted to let her go again.

"Captain Harris, I had not expected to see you so soon," Anjou said with a smile.

"I was about to leave for Merton."

"To visit me?"

"I am fortunate I ran into your sisters."

"We were just inviting him for tea," Jolie explained.

"May we walk take the long walk back through the park?" Anjou asked.

"Certainly. We will be behind you directly," Margaux replied with a mischievous grin.

Edward held out his arm and Anjou placed her hand on it, sending echoes of pleasure through him. He was close enough to smell her scent of bergamot, and it took much restraint not to pull her into his arms there in the middle of the street.

"Are you well, Edward?" she asked.

"I am very well now," he said, smiling down at her.

She smiled back at him. "I wish I had news from my father. Perhaps he will be at home."

"I have heard from your father. He paid me a visit last evening. In fact, he had charged me with delivering a message to you."

They stopped as they reach the corner of Piccadilly and she turned to look up at his face. "Do not leave me in suspense! Did the Bishop grant me the annulment?"

"He did."

"Oh, thank God," she said with both visible and audible relief.

They crossed the busy street to the park, and he noticed her sisters were lagging far behind, for which he was grateful. He led her away to a quiet bench, where they sat and he took both of her hands in his.

"Anjou, I had hoped for a better place to say this, but I am too impatient. Will you do me the greatest honour of becoming my wife?"

"I am surprised you needed to ask," she said coyly. "I was ready long before."

"Seven thousand years ago?" he asked with a raised brow.

"Precisely."

"I do need to warn you I made a deal with your father."

"I beg your pardon?"

"Apparently, your mother loves to throw grand parties."

Anjou groaned. "No, no, no!"

"I am afraid so, my love. Your sisters and brothers cheated her of lavish weddings and opulent parties in their honour."

"I might never forgive you for this," she cried.

She stood up and began to walk down a path in the trees. That was certainly not the response he expected. He hurried after her to reassure her.

"Where are you going? I am certain we may work something out with your mother."

She spun around. "You have no idea what you are up against,

Edward."

"I suppose not, but what could I say?"

She stopped and folded her arms across her chest. "Nothing. There was nothing else you could do. But I expect you to make it up to me."

"Every day of my life," he said with a huge grin as he took her in his arms and pulled her close. "Starting now," he muttered as he lips covered hers and he proceeded to grovel in a very satisfactory manner.

Epilogue

Fortunately, October weddings were a rarity in London. They had been able to book St George's for three weeks from the first calling of the banns. Lady Ashbury had spared no expense, and had invited every person of her acquaintance to the breakfast. Anjou was the shy one, yet here she was, being the one forced to endure the large gathering at the fashionable chapel. She did remember another St George's most fondly, so she had refrained from protest, thinking it a good omen.

Anjou sat in the vestibule, waiting for her father to come for her, since her hair had been styled and her gown had been donned long ago. Her sisters and mother had taken their places. Again she found herself waiting and impatient to have done. Her stomach churned at the thought of having so many people with their eyes upon her.

Her mother had surprised her by acquiescing to her wish for the guests witnessing the marriage ceremony to be limited to close acquaintances. The chapel had been adorned with simple ribbons and flowers on each pew, and the music was performed by a string quartet at Anjou's request. Her dress was fashioned from cotton of the faintest hint of blue, and adorned with satin stitch and gathered high above her waist. She had chosen to have her hair gathered loosely at her neck, with a simple tiara of silk forget-me-nots and a few tendrils to soften her face.

A knock on the door signalled it was time. She took a deep breath. "Enter."

Her father's face peered around the door and he smiled. "Are you ready?"

"I am." And she was.

"I received a letter for you, and I have been pacing back and forth trying to determine if I should wait until after the ceremony."

"Is it urgent?"

"I don't know. It is from Bermuda." He answered with hesitation.

"I suppose you should let me see it. As long as I am not late for my wedding!"

"I will watch the time." He handed her the letter and stepped outside to give her privacy.

She glanced down at the scrawl in Aidan's hand and also debated the wisdom of opening it before the ceremony, but she decided to go ahead. She broke the seal and read his words.

Lady Anjou,

After you left Bermuda, small pieces of my memory began to come back to me. Seeing you again must have triggered them. I sought out the advice of a doctor here and he believed you must have known me in England. My wife finally confessed the whole to me, and I wanted to express both my regrets and my gratitude. I cannot imagine what you must have felt when you saw your husband married to someone else, and that after having searched and waited many years. I am deeply sorrowed by this, and I do hope you will find happiness again. Something tells me you will. I am grateful for the love you had for me. I hope in time I will remember all of our time together and treasure it always.

Your loving,

Aidan

She had to wipe the tears away swiftly, for her father was knocking on the door. This was not the time to cry, but she was glad she had read the letter. It gave her some small measure of peace to know Aidan remembered her and had freed her.

She checked her appearance in the mirror one last time, more certain than ever that she was doing the right thing.

She was nervous as she stood at the entrance to the chapel. The red-carpeted aisle seemed longer than it ever had before, but when she saw Edward standing there, waiting for her at the altar, she locked her eyes with him to keep herself calm. From the corner of her eye she could see her sisters and their husbands, also Charles and Sarah, and finally her mother, who was dabbing at her eyes. When they reached the apse, her father wiped away tears too as he handed her to Edward.

The Reverend began with "Dearly beloved," and Anjou heard very little other than "I will," which was all she needed to know. She somehow managed to repeat her vows, kneel for prayers and sign the register. The only time she had almost lost her composure was when Edward placed the ring on her finger. He had selected a brilliant sapphire surrounded by diamonds in the shape of a forget-me-not. She had inhaled the start of a sob, when Edward had lifted her chin to reassure her. His eyes were again the mossy-green hue she had come to recognise as happiness. It was too much to fully comprehend, but nothing had ever felt so right.

~*~

The wedding breakfast was where her mother had her *coup d'é·tat*. The *Ton* was in full force for the show, which Anjou did not mind so much. She could remain safely by Edward's side and not be the sole centre of attention. There were lavish displays of food, flowers and fountains as society had come to expect from Lady Ashbury. The only small requests

225

Anjou had made were for the crew of the *Wind* to be invited, and for a rhubarb pie to be served. It was a jolly time, especially when she had presented Edward with a new violin she had commissioned on the day he proposed to her in London. The look he gave her made her wish the guests were gone. However, much to the members of the *Beau Monde's* dismay, they treated the crowd to a few sea shanties and songs she had learned at sea. Even Charles and Sarah joined in the dance. It was a part of who they were and seemed a fitting farewell to *With the Wind,* and the beginning of their new life—along with their new clowder of cats and a valet named Connors.

Preview of After the Rain...

"I regret to inform you, *mademoiselle,* that you must leave the school at the end of the term next week. There are no more charitable funds left after your mother's funds ran out, and you must admit the school has been very gracious."

"*Oui, madame,*" Christelle said as she kept her eyes downcast.

"I am very sorry, Christelle. I have kept you as long as I could, but the board feels you are old enough now to provide for yourself. I will draw up a list of potential employers for you to consider."

Christelle nodded her head. What choice did she have? Madame Thérèse was the only one who had ever shown her true kindness.

"I saved a trunk of your mother's effects for you," the headmistress said warily.

Christelle's head shot up in surprise.

"We did not feel it appropriate to give to you at the time. Perhaps it may be of use to you now." The woman pointed towards an old dusty trunk with leather straps and brass tacks. She then left the room and the door shut with a click.

It had been six years now since Christelle had been deposited on the doorstep of the Harriot school for girls in Paris, the day her mother had left for England. Her mother had gone to find someone after Monsieur Clement died, but she never returned. She had perished in a horrible accident in London, Christelle had been told, the day she discovered she was orphaned.

Christelle would not miss the school. She had been merely tolerated there due to her circumstances, and there were always whispers about her mother's occupation. She was no fool. She knew exactly what her mother had done to survive after her English husband had abandoned her. She had married Monsieur Clement, who had taken her in when she was desperate and penniless. He had done her no favours.

Christelle may bear his name, but he had been no father to her. She looked nothing like him and he had no love for her. Her mother had kept her away from him as much as possible.

When the other girls left for holidays, Christelle was the one left behind with the teachers who had no family to visit. Instead of kindness or affection, she was treated more as a servant. She was there on charity, after all.

But where would she go now? What would she do? There were no respectable jobs open to a girl with no connections or references. Was she destined to follow in her mother's footsteps? Christelle knew what to do. One did not live with the most beautiful woman in Paris without observing and learning.

She knew she was beautiful, for it was a source of scorn amongst fellow students. But she had not her mother's confidence.

Christelle looked out from the tiny window viewing over the rooftops to the Seine and the Notre Dame. It was a cold, dreary day, and it felt foreboding of being cast into the streets with nothing to her name. Could they not have spared her a spring eviction at least? A white pigeon landed in front of her on the windowsill, cocking its head around, looking lost.

She placed her hand slowly against the pane and the bird pecked at it.

"I have no food for you little one," she said sadly. "Soon there will be no food for me if I cannot think of something quickly."

The bird flew away, and she turned and eyed the trunk warily.

It only took a few short steps in her tiny attic room to reach the familiar old chest of her mother's. She had thought all was lost of her. Christelle ran her hand lovingly through the dust that had settled on it to find the initials LAS. She traced the letters with her finger and wondered why she had never known anything of her mother's family. There had literally been no one to turn to when her mother died. But then, they had not planned for her to die so young.

She undid the buckled strap and lifted the lid slowly. Her nostrils were assailed with a mixture of cedar and her mothers fragrance of roses. Sadness threatened to overwhelm her as she picked up the last garment she had seen her mother alive in. It was a bright Jonquil silk, and she recalled quite vividly helping her mother put stitches into it. Her mother had been a gifted seamstress and had taught Christelle to sew as early as she could remember.

She began to pilfer through her mothers beautiful gowns, and ideas of how she could rework them for her own use began to form. Perhaps they would be considered risqué for a young girl, but the dresses were the height of fashion at the time in Paris. Christelle wondered if her talents with needle and thread might be her only hope of survival for the near future.

At the bottom of the trunk she found some of her own things. A small stuffed doll she had carried everywhere as a child. She picked it up and held it to her cheek and the tears of longing for her mother streamed down her cheeks. She squeezed the doll tight and felt something hard inside. Christelle pulled it away from her body and begin to examine it. There had been nothing inside when she was a child, she was certain of it. She found some small stitches that had been placed on a seam.

She took a small pair of scissors from her sewing kit and cut open the new seam before digging through the stuffing for the object. When her fingers reached it, she pulled out what appeared to be a signet ring. It was made for a large man, of gold with a black onyx at the center of a crest.

Christelle had no idea who it belonged to. She had never seen it. Had her mother stolen it? Worse, had she received it as payment for her services? Christelle did not wish to think on it. However, she might need it to survive. She placed it safely back in the doll and re-stitched the seam.

Turning back to the trunk, she saw only a small leather journal in the bottom. She picked it up cautiously, unsure if she was ready to know its contents. She decided she would save it for later after she was resettled. She began to place it back in the trunk when a small yellowed piece of paper slipped out.

Christelle turned it over and read it.

Rosalind Christine Stanton
Born the Fifth day of February in the year Eighteen hundred ten
to Benedict Thomas Stanton and Lillian Adele Stanton

Christelle fell back on her haunches. "Is this me?"

Thank you for reading *With The Wind*. I hope you enjoyed it. If you did, please help other readers find this book:

1. Share the book with a friend who you think might like it so she or he can discover me, too.
2. Help other people find this book by writing a review.
3. Sign up for my new releases at www.Elizabethjohnsauthor.com, so you can find out about the next book as soon as it's available.
4. Come like my Facebook page www.facebook.com/Elizabethjohnsauthor or write to me at elizabethjohnsauthor@gmail.com

Other Titles by Elizabeth Johns:

Surrender the Past

Seasons of Change

Seeking Redemption

Shadows of Doubt

Second Dance

Through the Fire

Melting the Ice

First Impressions

About the Author

Like many writers, Elizabeth Johns was first an avid reader, though she was a reluctant convert. It was Jane Austen's clever wit and unique turn of phrase that hooked Johns when she was 'forced' to read Pride and Prejudice for a school assignment. She began writing when she ran out of her favourite author's books and decided to try her hand at crafting a Regency romance novel. Her journey into publishing began with the release of Surrender the Past, book one of the Loring-Abbott Series. Johns makes no pretensions to Austen's wit, but hopes readers will perhaps laugh and find some enjoyment in her writing.

Johns attributes much of her inspiration to her mother, a former English teacher. During their last summer together, Johns would sit on the porch swing and read her stories to her mother, who encouraged her to continue writing. Busy with multiple careers, including a professional job in the medical field, writing and mother of small children, Johns squeezes in time for reading whenever possible.

Acknowledgements

There are many, many people who have contributed to making my books possible.

Tracy and Brandie—my publicist and agent—I have never had so much fun researching!

I am grateful to the crew of the *Pride of Baltimore II* for allowing me to sail, and to Phil for showing me around the kitchen and graciously answering my many questions!

My family, who deals with the idiosyncrasies of a writer's life that do not fit into a 9 to 5 work day.

Dad, who reads every single version before and after anyone else—that alone qualifies him for sainthood.

Wilette, who takes my visions and interprets them, making them into works of art people open in the first place.

Karen, Tina, Staci, Judy, Shae and Kristiann who care about my stories enough to help me shape them before everyone else sees them.

Tessa and Heather who help me say what I mean to!

And to the readers who make all of this possible.

I am forever grateful to you all.

Made in the USA
Middletown, DE
17 February 2023

25106874R00142